Hear Me Out

T.K. Richards

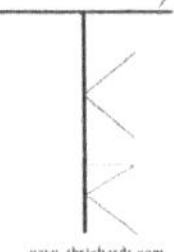

Note From The Author

A portion of this story was featured as six episodes entitled "PREY" on Kindle Vella in 2021 under a pseudonym I was testing as Triv Jones. Since then, the story has changed dramatically and has been adapted into this novella. The themes remain the same, but the names of the main characters have changed.

Thank you.

Content Warning

This novella contain mature themes and intended for mature audiences. Warnings of violence and multiple categories of abuse. Please view the trigger warnings below before proceeding.

The intent of this story is to bring awareness of sensitive subject matter.

WARNING: Psychological manipulation, sexual assault, emotional abuse, verbal abuse, physical abuse, stalking, and murder. Mentions of alcohol, weapons, drugs, sexual health, and violent acts.

I cannot play myself again,
I should just be my own best friend,
Not fuck myself in the head with stupid men.

— AMY WINEHOUSE

PROLOGUE

Men have served as the pit and the peach of my life. And in those pits were toxic, treacherous, egotistical, abusive liars. Can something be done about this problem? So far, the answer is no.

After surviving manipulation, deceit, and pain from the hands of conniving men, I rose from the depths of despair to the peak of resilience. Though it took me some time to get where I needed to be.

The journey here was a rough one. Moments of joy were few and far between, with the toughest being lessons I wish the women in my family would have warned me about.

Nevertheless, I'm not alone when it comes to being on the receiving end of men's fuckery.

Women reach out to me daily, telling their tales of bad experiences with bad men. Moments and mistakes that have molded them in their journey of womanhood.

These are their stories.

~Sophia

Chapter 1

"Where were you?" Sean, scolds me with stern eyes.

I rush past her nearly tripping on my heels. "Has everyone arrived?"

"You're the last." She raises her brows. "What's going on?"

I exhale, holding a tissue to cover red blots of blood on my hand. "Tell the ladies I'm here, and we'll begin in ten minutes." I lift the paper and flash the stains for her to see. "I'll explain everything after we wrap. Give me ten minutes to change my top, and I'll be ready."

From a private room tucked away in the corner of my studio, I catch my breath while observing three brave, beautiful women, sit at my round table. They've accepted my invitation to share intimate details of their past for an audience in search of healing and community—the reason I do what I do.

Moments prior to my arrival, I was inches away from death, but it wasn't my time to punch that clock. I can't say the same for the dead guy in the back seat of my car.

I shake off the visuals of my knife piercing his neck, as blood runs from my fingers down the drain. I convince myself the water removes my sins as I scrub my hands clean. Once they're dry, I'm given a clean slate.

I place my soiled shirt in a bag for disposal later, then pull a light zipper-neck sweater over my head and fluff my curls back in place. The ghost of a man walks past the camera, but his presence doesn't startle me. I'm not easily shook in my line of work and have gotten used to apparitions following me from time to time. I assume this one will linger until I atone. He's not the first and definitely won't be the last.

None of the ladies in the other room see him. Not even Sean, the best sister and yin to my yang— the only person that knows my secret.

She adjusts the height of the microphones in front of our guests while I compare what they look like in person to their online profiles. Mona Lisa is just as I imagined based on the pictures she posts on her timeline—short, pudgy, and petite with overpowering makeup packed on her yellow skin. Heavy lashes curl long enough to hide her eyes from the world. I wonder if that's by choice. Does she have a huge interest in cosmetics, or is it how she masks her inner feelings? I'll have my answer once I hear her testimony.

She tosses her brown coifs with a shift of her shoulder, pressing her painted red lips together, while Sean tightens the microphone on the stand. Deja, our second guest, extends her hand to Mona Lisa. I observe them introducing themselves, mesmerized at Deja's athletic build when she removes her jacket.

Her arms are lined to perfection. I'd expect nothing less after scrolling through her fitness website. Her beauty is magnetic: soft facial features, natural curves, ample bottom, and perfect smile. Her bohemian vibe, chunky jewelry, and sistaloc'd hair match the earthiness of her complexion and caramel-coated lips. I sense she's happy and in tune with herself.

Kylah, the tallest of the three melanated beauties, exudes an unapologetic-ness about her. Her nude lips match her conservative style, and her designer fitted suit says she's doing exceptionally well. She unbuttons her blazer then lifts her hand to scratch her serious face. But that could be a defense for a gentle soul. She is here after all.

She manages to squeeze out a smile when she shakes the hands of the other panelists. Secretly, she cleans her hands with a sanitation wipe in her purse then nervously fumbles with her long earrings that stop above her shoulder and end where her bob lays straight.

As the ladies chat, I close my laptop and beg for forgiveness, for they know not what they are about to giveth. They are innocent to my agenda, just as they were years ago in their youth when men manipulated and violated them—the theme of today's show.

I join the ladies sitting between the purple walls with pink and gray décor that helps bring a sense of calm to the set. Colors that relax the soul when discussing heavy topics, like we are about to do.

"So lovely to meet you all." I greet each one of them with a handshake.

Sean places bottles of water in front of them. "Ladies, remember if you want anything like tea, coffee, juice, soda, or a snack...I'll be happy to accommodate you." Her hand taps my arm. "I'll leave you to it."

Sean exits and dims the light in the room. The ghost disappears into thin air when the red recording sign on the wall glows behind me. I settle in, sip some apple juice, then clear my throat as a nervous energy travels around the table.

Raising my brows to Kylah, Deja, and Mona Lisa, I assure them, "This is a safe space."

They nod at me in unison.

I exhale. "Stand by. Roll sound. Sophia Mally. *Hear Me Out*. Episode 101. Title: *'The Manipulation of the Young Female Mind & How It Relates to Violence Against Women.'* Recording now."

Podcast: Hear Me Out
Host: Sophia Mally
Episode: 101

<u>Sophia</u>

Today we speak with victims who can attest to the manipulation of young women and different forms of violence girls and women alike experience in today's world. You will hear triggering testimony our guests have agreed to share in our efforts to bring awareness. Three brave women have come forward that share a common goal: knowledge of unhealthy relationships and how to navigate your exit, safety precautions while dating, and recognition of the different forms of abuse. Our panelists are

Kylah Sims, Deja Scott, and Mona Lisa
Whitmore. Welcome to *Hear Me Out.*

<u>Kylah</u>
Thank you for having us.

<u>Deja</u>
Yes. Thank you.

<u>Sophia</u>
How are you all doing today?

<u>Mona Lisa</u>
I'm a little nervous.

<u>Kylah</u>
So am I, but other than that, I'm doing great. I
feel like a weight is already being lifted from my
shoulders just by being here.

<u>Sophia</u>
Sharing your experiences has the power to reach
those that are silent or who have been silenced.
It's amazing how many lives can be touched by a
person's testimony. I personally want to thank
you for coming on today to tell us your stories.

<u>Kylah</u>

Thank you for opening up your platform to us. I'm sure I speak for all of us when I say we hope our stories will inspire the rising generation of women to make hard decisions that will better their lives.

Sophia
I couldn't agree with you more.

Deja
Society continues to place the blame of other's actions on the victim. Women are often labeled the responsible party when they have been victimized, preyed upon, and manipulated. And the majority of those victims are teen girls and new-adult women. It's time that changes.

Sophia
Well said. Ladies and gents joining us out there tonight, remember if you want to reach out and spread words of kindness or encouragement to our guests, please do so on our social media platforms. And remember, we delete negative comments, so don't waste your time. We are all about love and light on *Hear Me Out*. Kylah, would you like to begin with your story?

(Kylah sighs)

Kylah
Why not.

(Sophia nods to her producer)
Sophia
Ladies and gents of the *Hear Me Out* family, I present Ms. Kylah Sims.

Kylah
One last question: may I speak freely?

Sophia
By all means, the floor is yours.

Part I.

KYLAH

CHAPTER 2

KYLAH

To be young and reckless is a choice. A part of my growing pains was learning that such behavior casted me in the middle of a story I have come to regret and has haunted me for years.

To the young girls listening to my voice, I hope my story prevents you from making the mistakes I made. To the mothers listening today, raise your daughters to love themselves so they won't be flattered by the likes of anyone who shows them attention. Teach them that sometimes you'll be noticed by a cute face and tight body, but that doesn't mean you should engage. Attention comes at a price, and as my late grandmother used to say, "It ain't all it's cracked up to be." She also said, "Looks aren't everything." And she was right.

It took me a while to understand what my grandmother meant by that. I was young and thought I *knew* everything, as most teenagers do. I also heard what I wanted to hear—especially from men.

And I quote, "Tell your friends, they can get with my friends. And we can do this every weekend." Puffy~1994

These were words we lived by while pretending to be grown and on our own. Somehow paying our rent when our money was spent, working eight-dollar-an-hour jobs, going to school between shifts, living off campus in less-than-stellar apartments, and partying with celebrities—thinking this was the life because we didn't know any better. To put it mildly, we were stupid.

What kept us afloat? The dealers. Big time and small. One of the crew threw some ass one way for our party supply. Another one of us would give up the goods to round up the missing rent. And another toyed with men's affections and used her Coca-Cola-shaped body for whatever hookup we needed: private parties, VIP tickets, studio time, whatever.

My position? Tolerate Aston, also known as, Mr. Small Time. The short but cute, watching-paint-dry lay for grocery money and occasional free meals when the money ran out.

Aston was nice. He never disrespected me and always came through in a clutch, but he had a lot of whores on his team.

He downplayed me as his *homegirl* whenever I

popped up to his apartment for some money. I didn't mind. He wasn't my man, but whenever I needed anything, he held me down, and I never let any of the women on his roster know he was sleeping with me too.

Somewhere in the matrix, Aston got left behind. After losing contact with him, I met Egypt, a big-timer from Texas with business in *Cashville*—it's what we called Nashville because a lot of money was being made around our way.

I ran errands for Egypt. I chauffeured artists, tended to his list of girlfriends, and handled pickups here and there and whatnot. Doing whatever was necessary to make extra bank: delivering jewelry, clothes, shoes, and product to keep his ladies and clients happy.

Our relationship was strictly platonic. I did my job, got paid under the table, and earned other perks not worth mentioning.

One particular visit, he and his main chick were on the outs, and like the playbook says, we went friend for friend. I introduced him to one of my roommates, and he returned the favor the next time he came into town. And that's how I met Clay Anthony.

Ugh, if there was any way I could have foreseen the lessons coming my way when I met him, I would have never agreed to go to Egypt's apartment that night.

Clay had a baby face, head full of curly hair, and a nice build. My preference at that time was a tall, dark, and handsome good-time boy with fast money. Clay was the complete opposite, light-skinned, one inch taller than me, and so quiet at times I'd forget he was on the phone. But he was cute. I hate to give him that credit.

We hit it off, exchanged numbers, and built a long-distance something. I'm not sure what to call it. After I tell you my story, you'll see why I can't label it. But whatever it was, he gave me the nickname, Shor. And I loved to hear him call me that. The cadence of which he spoke neglected to sound out the 'ty' in shorty, and so "Shor" is who I was to him, and the term of endearment won me over after a while.

When he wasn't on mute, he said all the things a girl wants to hear. And coming from a cutie on a winning team, I gave him a shot—long distance, of course. Translation: I was still doing my thing in Tennessee, because I knew he was doing his thing in Texas. I had my flaws, but I wasn't naïve to think a guy like him didn't have options. And he rolled with my good friend Egypt who wouldn't know what the word monogamy meant if it were tattooed on his forehead.

Anyway, life went on, and business continued as

usual. Drops were made, dates were had, and parties were attended. *Sometimes*, the party followed us home as I ignored advice given to me by my grandmother.

"Don't let your house be the party house," she'd say.

A few days later, following that mistake, regret lurked outside my bedroom window. Shadows of two men in baseball caps appeared through the blinds. Their exaggerated silhouettes darkened my wall as the patter of a gun tapped on the glass and put the fear of God in me.

I screamed, and the perpetrators fired a shot into the siding as they fled, just missing my window. My roommates ran into my room, finding me frozen with tears trickling down my face.

Shock prevented me to speak at first, but when I was finally able to explain what I saw, we called Gina's boyfriend, Diaz, over to spend the night with us, though we never went to sleep.

The fear in us wanted to call the police, but we weren't police-calling people, not to mention we had drug paraphernalia and illegal substances stashed inside the house. So, we rotated night shifts instead, and wore ourselves thin, too afraid to go to sleep with faceless foes on the loose.

Days later, I received a message from Gina while

keeping my word to pick up the free condoms from the infirmary.

I called her from the phone at the desk. "What's up? I'm picking up the stash as we speak. You didn't need to remind me."

Her heavy breaths on the line made the hairs on my neck stand up.

"Gina. You alright?"

She stuttered, "I-It-It's-all-gone."

"What's gone?"

"The stash. The money. Our clothes. Everything. We have to call the police, Ky. We have to," she cried.

"Hide the bongs and papers, then call them. I'm on my way."

I took my time getting home with more worries added to the pile. I already didn't have my part of the rent, Aston was nowhere to be found, and now we had to find a way to cover the cost of what had been stolen.

By the time I arrived, the police were long gone, and Elle, Gina, and Diaz all sat mute on the couch when I walked in.

"What did they say?" I asked.

Gina shrugged her shoulders. "They said this was done by someone we know. An inside job. They came in through the kitchen window. The screen was thrown in the bushes, and the window was wide open. Whoever did it planned this and unlocked that window for an easy return."

Elle cut her off. "Basically, we were set up."

I kicked the air with my feet. "I knew better than to have a party here. Does anybody have an idea who would do this to us?"

Diaz cut Gina off. "Y'all will never know who did this. Put your big-girl panties on and level up."

I rolled my eyes at him and stormed into my room. It was wrecked. The dresser drawers were pulled out, my mattress hung off the bed spring, broken glass from the picture frame of my flea market picture of '*Pretty Eyes*' covered the carpet in my room, and my Ralph Lauren travel bag with a stash of marijuana hiding inside was stolen.

One thing stuck out at me immediately after examining my room carefully. The robbers only stole my boy-ish clothing. All of my sneakers, furlough shirts, and graphic hoodies were swiped, but they left all of my stilettos, dresses, and high-heeled boots. It was clear the robbery was done by a male.

The ordeal heightened my paranoia, and everyone around me felt like a foe including Gina, Elle, and their boyfriends. I wondered if they were in cahoots and staged the whole thing, but I kept my suspicions to myself to keep the peace.

Sleepless nights and looking over my shoulder became unbearable by the end of the week. Unable to get past the trauma, I freaked out. I withdrew from school, left Gina and Elle stuck with my part of the rent until they found a new roommate, and moved to Texas with my aunt that lived half-hour in the suburbs away from Egypt and Clay's stomping grounds. And so began the nightmare of a lost little girl creating a laundry list of embarrassing decisions.

Immediately, I abandoned myself and my integrity. I looked to Egypt to give me a job. "Put me on," I begged him, but he refused. And he was right to. I was not prepared or ready for the real world.

In his eyes, I was coming from a hot situation and was too eager, but he used the excuse that I didn't know the area well enough to work and not get caught up. He did throw some cash my way, being the kind friend I knew him to be, but at the end of the day, I was on my own.

Clay, on the other hand, turned out to be nothing like he had presented himself to be when he came down to The Ville. He was a total fraud. He perpetrated being a big-timer, when in actuality, he was low ranking and *worked for* the big-timers. His bank was laughable compared to the real hustlers I knew growing up, and he was nowhere near Egypt's status.

After putting two and two together, I learned he was a corner boy hustling nickels and dimes. I secretly held this as a strike toward Egypt. He knew what he introduced me to and I looked at him with a side-eye going forward. That was my missed opportunity to walk away from both of them.

Being a fool, I didn't cut my losses. Not even when I learned that Clay didn't have his own place and couldn't do shit for me. Turns out I could have taken care of him, and he would have let me if I was a total dumbass.

Living closer allowed me to see the real him, but I looked past his flaws and ignored the flaming-red flags smacking me in the face. I fell for the guilt trip where men gaslight women whenever they recognize their new partner shares the same flaws as the former.

"It ain't fair, Shor. You can't bring that baggage from some other man you been fuckin' wit' and put that shit on me," he said. "We ain't all the same."

I fell for that bullshit, partially because he was right. Everyone is different and shouldn't be judged as a whole, but when it comes to men who get worse and worse as time goes on, a woman has to abandon what is fair and live by what is logical.

If women go into every new relationship and forget how their previous lover treated them or ignore trigger words they've heard before, then they would be susceptible to the same shit with the next man. And the cycle goes on and on until all hope is lost. I unfortunately found myself in that cycle down in Texas.

I was barely twenty years old, and hadn't figured out this methodical pattern males use to manipulate women. I was naïve, desperate to be loved due to daddy issues, and had a serious problem of wanting people to like me, like most girls do at that age. I was the perfect recipe for someone like Clay to do what he did to me.

Now, whenever I hear those famous words, *"I'm not him,"* and my absolute favorite, *"You're bringing old shit into new shit,"* my antennas rise like the phoenix to keep from making the same mistake twice.

To avoid confrontation, I chose not to confront him on the lies he sold me. I had been in an "alleged" long-distance relationship with a pathological liar living with an undiagnosed personality disorder and anger issues.

He would say he had to make a run out of town then later reveal he hadn't been anywhere, without realizing he was telling on himself, but I didn't call him out—at first.

He would count wads of money in front of me, alluding it was all of his earnings, when in actuality, it was money he had to turn in. Then, the user in him revealed its ugly head.

Clay called me one day while I was out shopping. "Shor, see if they got the new Scottie Pippen sneakers in my size before they sell out. I'll give you the 160 when I see you," he promised.

The best way to get me to turn on you is to mess with my money. I remember my skin itching and seeing my mother's face in my head when he asked the favor. She raised me on old-school catch phrases and Bible quotes, but also mottos of her own, and she was adamant that a woman is to never give a man money.

But I chose to ignore my intuition that was doing somersaults in my chest and go against everything I believed in and was taught, and I bought the sneakers like a fool.

When I saw him, I passed him the bag and held my hand out. He sucked his teeth at me.

"Girl, I'mma give you yo' money. Chill out."

I did just that. I chilled out until it was time for me to leave, still waiting on my money to be put in my hand.

Instead, I was sent packing with sixteen dime bags of weed to hand off to my cousin as a repayment of my money. Side note: you don't have to be romantically involved to get screwed over by a man, because I'm sure you have guessed, my cousin never gave me a cut of that money. Family *ain't* always family, but that's a different story for a different day.

Days later, Clay attempted to make me a corner

girl, probing me with questions about my family's business affairs.

I remember a chill traveling down my spine when he learned how much real estate my family owned. His face lit up brighter than the Christmas tree at Rockefeller Plaza, and he smiled bigger than I had ever seen him smile before.

That smile quickly transitioned into anger when I refused to ask my uncle to rent out one of his properties for cheap so Clay could turn it into a dope house.

Yeah, sure, I had dealings with dope boys. I wasn't innocent, but I wasn't stupid enough to hold someone else's product or take a charge for the team. Orange is not a good color on this Black woman, and I thank God the propaganda of being a ride-or-die chick never sold on me.

But still, the nasty attitude, and audacity of him conjuring up a plan to use me like that wasn't enough for me to wise up and distance myself from his antics. It was he who distanced himself from me when he didn't get his way. If my brain had been fully developed and I had been taught how to micromanage my emotions, I would have made sure our separation remained permanent at that point. Unfortunately, I still had some growing up to do.

Intermission 2

Kylah

I didn't think I would get emotional. Sorry.

Sophia

No need to apologize. Let's take a short break. *Hear Me Out* will be right back after this word from our sponsors.

(Kylah sips water)
Kylah

This is harder than I thought it would be.

Sophia

You're doing great, Kylah. We can take as many breaks as you need.

Kylah

Thank you. I just need a minute to catch my breath. Then, I'll be ready to continue.

Chapter 3

KYLAH

W e all make mistakes, but I don't consider my entertaining Clay a mistake. I consider it reckless, stupid, and the result of being what is known as *A Black Girl Lost*.

I'd survived him, wised up, and had been without his toxicity for nearly a month. And all it took was one phone call from him to dumb me down again.

"'Sup, Shor. You been M.I.A. lately. I ain't seen yo' number light my phone up in a minute."

A smart person would have sent his call to voice-mail, blocked his telephone number, hung up at the sound of his voice. But the lost little girl in me that lacked self-esteem and was desperate for attention, also weakened by a stupid nickname, allowed herself to be mind-fucked.

And why? I had no knowledge of self-worth and allowed emotion to lead me back into his trap. I could have volunteered my brain to undergo studies of how intelligence miraculously disappears for love —or whatever that feeling is when you think you've found it. But this wasn't that, because Clay didn't love me. I know that much. And I didn't love him. That became clear by the hate I felt toward him which superseded how I felt *for* him during our "relationship".

"You should come see me this weekend. Come see my new spot," he added.

I assumed he was finally becoming established and was eager to make the images I created of us in my head a reality. Images of me spending the night with him in a residence, not a cheap motel, and the two of us playing house like we discussed over late-night phone calls when two states were between us.

So, I forgave him and went to see his new place, hoping to eliminate my suspicion that he lived off other people.

Before both of my feet were fully in the door, I noticed a little girl stretched out on the couch.

"Shor, I got an important run to make to pick up some money. Can you sit with my little cousin for about thirty minutes?"

"What?" I scowled, struggling to understand his sob story. "You haven't even shown me around your new place."

"Look around by yourself, and tell me what you think when I get back."

Afraid to tell him no, I stood in silence and watched him walk out of the door with my dignity trailing behind him.

I sat in that apartment, pretending everything was okay to comfort the child that had control of the remote. She had no idea I was fuming as Clay's quick run turned into hours, and I had been played to provide a free service as a babysitter.

In the presence of her innocence, I sat across from her, thinking of ways I could kill her cousin—*if* she truly was his cousin.

I thought about how the sex was average, the shoes he swindled out of me that pained my chest every time I saw a pair of them on someone's feet, and how the weeks I hadn't heard from him were actually delightful.

An image of Redd Foxx calling me a BIG DUMMY danced in my head all night. And finally, I made up my mind that I was done with this clown.

Keys jingled at the front door the next morning. I stood up ready to leave, and lash out at Clay, but was met with a mirrored reaction.

"Who the hell are you?" The woman scowled.

My brows furrowed. "Who are you?"

"Excuse me, lil' girl?"

Nervously, I replied, "I'm Clay's girlfriend."

"I swear that boy ain't shit. I gave him a place to stay if he promised to do one thing for me, and he got my baby in the house with a complete stranger." She seethed, rolling her eyes.

"I'm sorry. I didn't know. I was just helping him out. I fed your daughter one of the frozen lasagnas last night and gave her a popsicle before she went to bed. I'll fold up this blanket and be on my way."

The woman watched me from the corner of her eye as I tidied up where I slept. My blood was boiling with madness, but the red color flushing my face was no match for the embarrassment I felt for believing Clay had changed. And to think that he had done so for me was the biggest fantasy I had ever invented.

The woman shared that she was his aunt, the child I watched was her daughter, and confirmed my suspicion that he was indeed living in someone else's house and lied to me yet again.

"Sorry to have bothered you," I said to the mother.

"Wait a minute before you go." She reached in her purse and handed me forty dollars. "Here. For your trouble." She wiggled the money until I took it.

"It really was no problem. You don't have to pay me."

"I'm gonna do more than pay you. I'm gonna help you." Her voice lowly roared with warning. "You seem like a nice girl. Leave my no-good ass nephew alone. You hear me? I meant what I said a minute ago. He ain't shit. He's a bum. He won't work, he won't clean, and he goes from house to house to whoever in the family will let him stay until he wears out his welcome."

Covered in shame, I asked her, "So, whose car does he drive?"

"Anybody dumb enough to let him hold one," she scoffed. "And right now, I'm the dummy."

I didn't blink. I had never been given a direct, negative, or accurate description of a person I was dating, as the one Clay's aunt gave of him. She spoke with such conviction that I believed every word she said, and I'd never felt more humiliated.

"Thank you for telling me." I tried to wipe the tears from my eyes before she saw it.

"I didn't mean to make you cry, sweetheart. But you needed to hear it. Find you someone with ambition. A *man*, not a little boy. My nephew will bring you down right along with him. I've seen it happen before."

"Yes, ma'am."

I left her house with tears streaming down my face, angry that I didn't listen to my instincts and upset about the fallacy I created in my head. I got down on myself and questioned what was wrong with me. Where was my self-esteem for the love of God?

It was apparent I didn't have any. I had fallen prey to a demon, and I'd fed myself a lie like other women—that I could change a man and turn him into the kind of man I wanted him to be. I could make him love me by doing whatever he asked of me. I could win him over by being nice, and kind, and understanding to his needs. And I ignored my inner voice and paid for it, as this wasn't the end of my ordeal with a true-born monster.

(Kylah wipes her eyes.)

<u>Sophia</u>
Let's take a short break.

CHAPTER 4

KYLAH

<u>Kylah</u>
Thank you for being patient with me. I didn't think I would cry today. I thought I had all of that out of my system.

<u>Sophia</u>
No one here is judging you.

<u>Kylah</u>
(She sips.)
A few more sips of water, and I'll be ready to pick up where I left off. This final part is where I hope to keep it together.

<u>Sophia</u>
Take your time. We're here for you. And with you.

<u>Kylah</u>
(She exhales a deep sigh.)
Where was I?

<u>Sophia</u>
You mentioned you ignored your inner voice.

Y ES. Never ignore that voice. That voice is your wisdom. Your guide. Your everything.

I didn't know that then. I could hear it speak to me clearly at times, telling me what I should and should not do, but I wasn't tapped in when I was younger, so I ignored it—as well as his aunt.

Clay called me after communication had been cold between us for nearly a month. I ruined my peace and abandoned my pride when I answered his call. It was as if he could sense I was doing fine without him. Like he could smell that I was happy, and he wasn't having any of that.

His laugh skipped like a scratched record when he said, "You let my aunt scare you off?"

"I don't know what you're talking about. She was nice to me."

"Then *how come* I ain't heard from you? What's been up *witchu*, stranger?"

"Working."

The phone went silent. He waited for me to do the usual—carry the conversation and serve myself up like a platter. But when I didn't, he was thrown off, not knowing what to make of the short answers I was giving him.

The lack of interest in my tone pissed him off.

"So, it's like *dat* now?"

I didn't answer him right away. I sighed, contemplating if my reply should be abrasive, or another one word response.

"*Whatchu* want, Clay?"

This is where I messed up. I should have hung up on him, or went with the abrasive comeback and said, "Yes, *it was like that now*," or "Fuck all the way off." I hate that the right words seem to come to me after the fact, but I digress.

He was taken aback by my question and held back his first response behind a minor groan. In his silence, I sensed a shift in his mood. He adjusted his bruised ego, ditched the growing frustration from his failed manipulation tactics, and played on my insecurity. He was smart. Cunning. Calculated.

"Look, Shor, I know you' mad at me right now, but come up and see ya man. We'll grab somethin' to eat, go see *dat* movie you was buggin' me to see, and chill after. Let me make it up to you."

Less than enthused, I replied, "I'll think about it."

"You do that."

I held strong and didn't call him back. I admit, it felt good to make him sweat for a change. To have *him* waiting to hear from me, and wonder if he would see me again.

By the weekend, his name lit up my phone, and the power of having him chase after me felt like a million bucks. I let his call go to my voicemail, and replayed his message over and over until I believed his apology for the way he'd treated me was sincere.

He called again, and I caved. I lied to my aunt that a few girls from work were going clubbing and having a sleepover after. She bought my story and was fine with the idea, expecting me back home the next day.

I felt bad having lied to her as I drove to see Clay, praying his aunt wasn't there to call me out on my stupidity.

To this day, I wish I could take back that prayer. *She should* have been there. I wish she *was* there. Because her presence could have saved me from what happened once I arrived.

(Kylah takes a deep breath)

<u>Sophia</u>
Take a minute.

<u>Kylah</u>
Thanks, but no thanks. I'd like to continue and get it all out.

<u>Sophia</u>
Then, by all means, please, whenever you're ready.

BEFORE I continue, I should warn you that what I am about to share is not easy for me to relive. And I want to reiterate to young girls that I am sharing my story in hopes none of you will go through what I went through.

I have called myself stupid, and for years thought I was the dumbest girl on the planet because of the horrible decisions I made when I was younger. I had faith in everyone, which was naïve of me, because bad people can smell innocence a mile away. Please remember that.

Lastly, no matter the circumstance, you should never drive to see a man. If he likes you, he'll come to you. And you should be worth that.

I arrived to the apartment, dressed to impress in a cute summer dress and low-heeled sandals, with my hair pulled back in a braided ponytail, excited Clay was making an effort. I remember how happy and jittery I felt the closer his footsteps made it to the door.

But all that good energy I brought with me was instantly drained when his drunk friend, Sling, opened the door, smiling at me like a creep.

"What's up, girl?" He moved to the side. "*Clay in the back.*"

The sight of Sling made my blood boil, and my instincts told me to turn around and go home, but I forced my stalled feet to cross over into the apartment. Once again ignoring that little voice that protects us.

I scoffed, thinking to myself, *'What's up, girl?' He doesn't remember my name.'*

Clay then walked up front, grinning at me on the side of his mouth as if he was the devil himself—not at all how I imagined he would greet me from his apology.

I didn't know what to make of his friend being at the apartment on the night of our "date," so, I half-smiled back at him.

He wrapped his hands around my waist. "You look real nice, Shor."

"Thank you. Are we doing a double-date thing or...?"

He scowled. "What you talkin' 'bout?"

My eyes shifted toward Sling.

The two of them shared a menacing look, snickering. Discomfort is an understatement of how I felt in the room with them. Every hair on my body prickled, and so I attempted to be clever and changed the subject.

"I feel overdressed. Where else are we going besides the movies?"

"Damn, Shor, why you trippin' on my gear?"

"I'm not." I finagled out of the argument he was trying to pick—or so I thought I was—and pointed to my bag. "Well, I brought clothes to spend the night. I can change into something less dressy."

Clay's body language changed from tense to antsy. His charade came to an end, and the person hiding below the mask he wore when I walked in exposed himself.

"Me and Sling gonna step out for a minute. Me and you'll do our thing when I get back," he said, sticking his chest out.

I breathed through his intimidation and spoke calmly with a trembling voice. "That's alright. You two go ahead and do your thing. I'm gonna head out and will catch you another night."

I adjusted my bag and turned for the door. A sudden waft of air blew on my neck, and a tug on my hair pulled me backward.

"Naw, Shor. You *gon'* be here when I get back." Clay snatched my keys from my hands and threw my ninety-eight-pound body to the floor.

I sat on my hands and knees in disbelief as he hovered over me, bracing myself to be struck.

I was too afraid to look at him, so I kept my head down and my eyes low. They were leveled with his thighs, positioned directly in front of my face. His fists were balled tight, turning red from the pressure, and fear ushered out all of the joy I had when I arrived.

I shrunk lower to the floor and made eye contact with Sling. It was soul crushing to find he didn't have a care in the world about Clay handling me with such malice.

He looked me dead in my eyes and said, "Clay, man, let's go."

I felt like the last breath of fresh air had been pulled from me. In moments like that, you don't know what to do. Do you risk fighting back and upset your abuser who can escalate his blows and inflict more pain? Or do you stay down and pray the strikes are over?

I had so much rage in me from the months of being misled, lied to, toyed with, and humiliated, that it got the best of me. So, I stood my ground. But Clay overpowered me with ease, forcing me to submit as he wrestled me back to the floor.

He pulled my mangled purse off my arm, dug inside it for my cell phone, put it in his pocket, then dragged me by my arms halfway toward the balcony.

I kicked and squirmed until I broke free and watched him open the sliding doors where he threw my purse and bag seven floors down into the bushes.

Horrified he was going to throw me next, I jumped up and ran past Sling through the front door.

"Help me!" I screamed to a man rolling his bike into the elevator a few feet ahead. "Hold it for me! Please!" I yelled, sprinting toward him.

The man looked back at me and rolled his bike inside the pulley. I ran up to the open doors and stuck my hand between them, looking at the man pressing the button for it to close. Clay's hands yanked my hair and pulled me back as the doors shut in my face and dragged me back into the apartment as I kicked and screamed for one of the neighbors to help me.

My faith in humanity was lost in that moment. I would never be able to pick out that man in the elevator in a lineup, but to this day, I roll my eyes at the sight of the football team that was on his gray cap. I remember his cropped denim jacket, an earring in his right ear, and his emotionless, dark face pushing that button with one hand and the other gripping the handlebar on his bike.

I kicked and screamed, burning my calves with carpet rash, further infuriating Clay as he lugged me back into the apartment. Defeated and lifeless from shock, he threw me down to the black-and-white checker-tiled floor of his aunt's office like a rag doll, and locked me inside.

The devastating click of the door stayed with me for a long time. It was a haunting sound. Something you'd never imagine could affect you, yet trouble you as simple as it is.

I lay on that hard floor and cried like a newborn. I can't remember how long I lay there in disbelief, but it was for a good while until I had come to terms that I wasn't stuck in a bad dream. I was actually living in a nightmare. I thought, *This can't be happening to me. Not me.* And it all happened so fast.

I held myself in a ball on the floor until the hardness of the tile became unbearable. Trapped, I paced in circles, occasionally looking out a tiny rectangular window, wide enough for an arm to wave out of it— too small for a body to squeeze through.

The office was filled with boxes in every corner. The desk was stacked with papers and folders and supplies. Out of boredom, I combed through his aunt's belongings with a racing mind, but distracting myself didn't stop my tears.

I cried until my chest hurt, sitting from box to box, then took my chances and rifled through his aunt's junk closet. I found more papers, books, and clothes stuffed in bags, and piled the contents together, making a soft place to sit on the floor, then stared at the bare walls for hours on the cusp of going insane.

I returned to the closet and uncovered a fax machine sitting in an old, wooden chair buried behind mounds of trash bags filled with baby clothes. The sight of it filled me with a glimmer of hope.

Frantically, I lugged the chair out of the closet, dragged the machine near the phone jack, and plugged the cord in the socket. I shuddered at the sound of a dial tone as faces of friends and family crossed my mind. Some were too far away to call, other's numbers failed me as I didn't remember them from having them saved by name, and the rest were people I couldn't rely to pour water on me if I was on fire—people like Clay, who should have been deleted from my life.

In that moment, I realized that if I made it out of that apartment alive, changes needed to be made. It was heartbreaking that my contacts were filled with people who I couldn't count on in a crisis, and I felt so alone.

I had no one to help me except my family. The aunt I lied to about my whereabouts, a cousin who had shitted me out of money and would exploit my ignorance for still being involved with Clay, and distant relatives who I always felt never really gave a damn about me—and who would further shame me for winding up in such a situation.

Desperation seeped in, leading me to swallow my pride and dial my cousin for help, but I hung up before the line rang, choking on that same pride when I could hear his laughs in my head. I also doubted he would show up.

Riddled with guilt, I sat there blaming myself, with no one to call, on the brink of a nervous breakdown. I heaved and contemplated dialing 911 even though I was raised to keep the authorities out of our business.

The image of my face being plastered on the news and the embarrassment it would bring to my family's name felt like a priority. And the hurt my lie would cause my aunt didn't sit well with me. She took me in, after all, when I was lost, down and out with nowhere to go, so I put the phone down, and waited it out.

The night carried on, and I padded the hard chair with the clothes, sitting with my thoughts, struggling to remember telephone numbers. The only ones I knew by heart were my friends' back in Nash.

Thinking of how they would have come to my rescue comforted me and kept me sane for a short while. That comfort disappeared as I rocked back and forth in that wooden chair, hating and blaming myself for agreeing to meet up with the devil after he'd already shown me his face.

I imagined his aunt looking down on me if she

found me battered, bruised, and locked inside her office after she warned me to steer clear of her nephew.

Being pitied and victimized infuriated me past the humiliation. And at the brink of dawn, my restlessness fueled my rage. I began guessing Egypt's phone number—disturbing many households regardless of the time.

I dialed several wrong numbers, but I was desperate. And after twenty or thirty attempts, Egypt's deep voice picked up the line.

"Who the hell callin' me this early?"

My voice cracked. "Egypt, it's me."

"Me, who?"

"Ky."

"'Sup, babes. Why you sound like that?"

Patiently, he waited for me to calm down and catch my breath to form clear sentences. I stumbled my way through a quick rundown of what Clay had done to me and was met with silence at first.

"Ky, come on, love. He *don't* really *gotchu* locked up in a room. You making all this shit up. Right?"

"No," my voice trembled. "I know you know where his aunt lives. Can you come get me? Please?"

"You serious, *ain'tchu*?"

I couldn't answer him. Hearing him question the seriousness of the matter caused me to relive everything Clay had done to me. Every moment of the ordeal. I grew hysterical, forced to accept this was reality, and unable to utter another word.

"Stop cryin', Ky. You makin' me feel like *I'mma have* to kill this motherfucka. Fuck is wrong with him? Damn! Just stop cryin'. I'll be there as soon as I can."

<u>Sophia</u>
This seems like a good time to take a break.

<u>Kylah</u>
Actually, if I take a sip of water, I'd like to continue and get it all out.

<u>Sophia</u>
Then, by all means, please continue when you're ready.

<u>Kylah</u>
Thank you.

Chapter 5

CHAPTER 5

___

KYLAH

I dozed off while waiting for Egypt to come to my rescue. When the sun was high in the sky, a sudden slam of the front door brought me to my feet.

I was sore from sleeping in the fetal position on stacked clothes spread across boxes against the wall, but I rushed to place my weight against the door, praying I'd hear Clay's aunt on the opposite side.

The handle jiggled, and the lock clicked. Violently, the door pushed open, knocking me to the floor.

Clay pulled my hair and dragged me into the living room. I didn't scream or fight him this time, thinking if I resisted, he wouldn't throw me over the balcony like he did my bags.

"You a lil' crafty bitch." He tossed me on the sofa. "How did you call Egypt?"

I placed my face between my knees and balled up on the couch as he cursed at me and mugged the top of my head. I shook, holding in my urine, afraid to move or open my mouth.

Sling walked through the front door and laughed. "Y'all two lovebirds still at it."

His joke pierced my soul. I was in the company of not one, but two devils, enjoying my torment.

Close to pissing on myself, I mustered up the courage to ask if I could use the bathroom. Clay ignored me and pulled an iron and ironing board out of the hall closet then turned the music up loud.

"Can I go to the bathroom?" I asked again.

No answer.

Sling sat on the lounge chair across from me and shouted over the music, "Let the girl go to the bathroom!"

Clay fanned his hand at me. "Go 'head."

After I relieved myself, I faced the mirror. I didn't recognize the girl staring back at me. Eyes the size of two gumballs, puffy and red. Hair all over the place like a rat's nest. I hated that girl and the one trapped inside of it. The foolish, lost idiot with no self-worth at the mercy of a lying, broke, corner boy.

The image in the reflection put a dark thought in my head. I saw myself jumping out of the window to end my life so I couldn't remember what I was experiencing. I wanted to die and be reborn to make better decisions. Erase my existence. Erase Clay.

I turned on the faucet, washed my hands, then splashed water on my face, stalling my return to the cruelty that awaited me in the other room.

Bang!

"*You*' been in there long enough! Open the door!" Clay kicked.

I'd had enough. I was tired. Done being thrown around like a rag doll. Distraught and furious that Egypt called Clay instead of showing up for me. I needed him there. He was my only friend close by, and the only person I trusted who would keep this a secret and spare what was left of my dignity.

Blood rushed to my head at the sound of his voice ordering me around, and something exploded inside of me. A sudden burst of adrenaline flushed through my body as I opened the door and threw everything from the counter at Clay—spraying his face with a can of spritz while kicking my way past him to the front door.

He trailed behind me, calling me every bitch he could think of. But this time, when he caught up to me, I fought back harder than I did the first time.

He wrestled me with one hand, rubbing his spritzed eyes with the other until we were back in the living room. He crowned my head with an open palm until my body lifted off the ground. The pain from the squeezing pressure felt like my brain was being suppressed into pieces.

I screamed and begged for him to stop, and he did, but not because I asked him to. But to bang it against the wall.

His other hand reached back and grabbed the iron sitting on the board. Clay held me up by my throat and positioned the hot iron near my face. When the steam hissed on my cheek, I gave up. I closed my eyes, stopped struggling, and accepted this was my end.

I didn't need to have eyes on him to see how he was enjoying the fear he put in me. I could feel it in my bones, hear it in his voice.

And in the face of evil, I began to think like evil. I said to myself that if he ruined my face and I didn't die, I would find a way to kill him. If I made it out of that apartment alive and unburnt, I would still kill him.

Standing there lifeless, the steam slightly cooled, and I met eyes with that asshole. The evil and delight in his eyes was something I had only seen in films. Never did I think I would witness such a thing myself or that it would be directed at me.

He laughed at the fright written on my face and said, "Wouldn't matter if I burned you. You ain't that pretty *noway*."

He slid me down the wall by my throat while the iron still seared in his other hand.

For the first time during my violation, I prayed, "Jesus, help me. God, I repent."

A knock interrupted whatever he was planning to do to me next.

"Clay, open up! I know *you in* there, man!" Egypt shouted through the door.

I remained tense at his mercy, hiding the relief I felt from the sound of Egypt's voice.

Clay's face seethed with anger. His laugh stopped. And with his tight grip around my neck gagging me, he put down the iron and covered my mouth.

"Shut the fuck up 'til he leaves," he ordered, then tugged on the hairs above the nape of my neck as he pushed me into his aunt's office.

The lock clicked, and I died inside. I lost hope that Egypt would get into the apartment and save me, and I questioned if my nightmare was finally over.

Clay's muffled voice echoed through the crack from the bottom of the door. I held my breath, waiting to hear the front door open.

"What the fuck you got goin' on in here, man?" Egypt said in the distance, but his deep voice sounded closer.

"*Why you* here, man? I told you we would get up later. I'm just getting in."

"Why is Ky's car banged up like that?"

"You came over here to talk about dat lyin' ass girl, man? I can't believe she called you with dat bullshit."

"Where she at?"

"She ain't here."

I banged on the door. "I'm in here! Egypt, please get me out of here!"

"The fuck is wrong with you, Clay! Open that fuckin' door and let that girl out! And to think I thought she was bullshittin'! You *done* lost your mothafuckin' mind!"

"This don't concern you, E. You need to leave."

"Boy, you know me well enough to know I *ain't* come over here alone. Ey! Dell and Ray! Get in here!"

The voices grew heavy beyond the door. I couldn't tell who was saying what as their voices bellowed on the other side, but the lock jiggled, and I shook from fear, not knowing who would be standing on the other side of it.

I backed away and lifted the fax machine from the floor as a weapon. Egypt opened the door and looked at me with horror in his eyes.

Slightly parting his mouth, he hummed low enough for me to hear him. "This crazy motherfucka done went too far." He placed one arm around me after I dropped the fax machine. "Come on. I gotchu."

Egypt escorted me out of the room, cursing Clay out as we walked toward the front door.

"Why did you do Ky like this, man? She always been good people! Look at her! Look at her fuckin' face!"

I kept my head down, not wanting to look at the likes of Clay ever again.

Dell stood at my other side. "You fuckin' crazy, dog. You need *yo'* ass whipped." He pointed at Sling. "And *you* just as fucked up to sit in here and not help this girl. Fuckin' punks."

I whispered to Egypt, "He has my keys. And he threw my purse and my bag over the balcony."

Dell sighed. "Say the word, E, and I'll lay this motherfucka out right now."

I clutched Egypt's hand.

"Let's get her out of here. Ray, see if you see somethin' out back."

Dell went to the balcony and confirmed he saw my things mixed in with the bushes while Egypt led me outside. I let go of his hand once we made it off the elevator and exhaled deeper than river water when we made it to my car.

It had been vandalized. The front window on the passenger side was bashed in. A single gunshot hole was in the back window, and the hood and the driver's door were beaten with countless dents.

People whispered as they walked by, staring at me and the car. Their reaction triggered tears to trickle down my face. I had been made a spectacle, the very thing I didn't want broadcasted on the news. A future face of women on a forgotten list nobody cares about.

Egypt consoled me. "I'm sorry that boy did this to you."

I know he was, but I had no words for him. I was thankful he came to my rescue, but I hadn't let go of the fact that he called him to verify my story. And while I had all night to wrestle with my thoughts and reflect on my horrific decisions, it had dawned on me that it was *he* who introduced me to this vile creature, and I wondered why he would do that to me if we were truly friends.

"You gonna be alright to drive?" Egypt asked me, pointing at the damage to my car.

"I have no choice." I wiped my eyes. "I ain't even supposed to be over here with him. My aunt thinks I went on a girls' trip this weekend. I gotta go home and explain this shit."

Dell spoke up on my behalf. "She don't need to be behind the wheel. Look at her shaking and shit. She can't drive."

Ray walked from around the building with my

bags. "Somebody need to handle ole boy for real. Where am I putting her stuff?"

"The backseat is fine," I said.

"Ray, drive her car to my crib." Egypt opened the back door of his truck. "You comin' home with me. I'll have one of my people fix your windows."

We rode in silence to his place, where his girlfriend provided me with a sweat suit she didn't mind parting with after I showered. She laundered the clothes I was wearing and from my bag, exceeding the amount of kindness I felt I didn't deserve bringing my drama into her house. And without knowing it, her charity and pity toward me, saddened me further as it sealed in the fact that I was a victim. Something I never aspired to be.

While I rested, Egypt's friend who owns a glass company repaired my windows. I called my aunt and lied to her about my whereabouts, spent the night in Egypt's spare room, thanked him in the morning for rescuing me, and left Texas.

For twelve hours, I blasted music and cried my way back to Nashville, only taking breaks to eat and rest. To stay awake, I occasionally drove with the windows down to feel fresh air blow on my face, rejoicing I was still alive.

Gina and Elle took care of me for a few days until the swelling in my face went down. Then I went to see my mother, who instinctively sensed something was off with me, even though my wounds were no longer visible.

It was something about being in her presence that made me cry like a baby. I didn't have to say a word, yet she knew something had happened to me and nurtured my spirit without my asking.

I never shared the details with her, but I know she whispered something in my brother's ear who popped over not long after my arrival. He called for me to join him as he inspected my car.

"How many times are you gonna make me ask you what happened here?"

"I don't know what happened to the car."

"I bought this car for you. We agreed you wouldn't let anyone else drive it, so what do you mean you don't know?"

"I wasn't there. It was like this when I made it outside."

"What you mean *made* it outside? Fuck happened to you?"

I wiped my tears and remained silent.

"Ky? You in some sort of trouble?"

"Not anymore. Can we just let this go? Please? It doesn't matter now. I made it home. I'll find a way to fix the car."

"Fuck the car. You gon' tell me what's going on and you gon' tell me right now."

I wanted revenge with every bone in my body,

but I wanted to be the one to carry it out. My brother didn't belong behind bars because of my dumb decision to get entangled with a jerk, but he begged me to give him what he needed to find him.

"Let me be the big brother that I am," he said. "The score has to be settled."

And I did. I showed him a picture of Clay that was stored in my phone and gave him the address of where my abuse took place.

"Promise Mama won't ever know about this."

He nodded, and we never spoke about it again. To this day, I have zero knowledge if my brother did anything to him on my behalf, and today is the very first time I've spoken about this since.

Intermission 3

Sophia

Kylah, I want to commend you for your bravery and for coming forward with your story. How do you feel after sharing it?

Kylah

I'm feeling a mixture of emotions. Shame. Anger. But mostly, I feel free and light.

Sophia

No need to feel shame. You are the victim. None of what happened is your fault.

Kylah

(She sips her water.)
Thank you, but I've always felt it was.

Sophia

Because society always places blame on a woman that's been victimized. These conversations are meant to change that. You chose to give that man a chance to redeem himself, and he chose violence. Not you.

Kylah

I know.

Sophia

Has your abuser ever tried to contact you?

Kylah

Not to my knowledge.

Sophia

I apologize in advance for this next question. Have you ever tried to contact him?

Kylah

No. But I did search his name online once.

Sophia

What were you hoping to find?

Kylah

I was hoping to see an obituary.

<u>Sophia</u>
And?

<u>Kylah</u>
Instead, I saw his face staring back at me through the screen. He still has those demonic eyes, and he looked like shit. But he was where he belongs--behind bars. I didn't look at the page long enough to know why he was incarcerated, though. Whatever it was, I'm sure he is guilty, and I'm just glad he was caught.

<u>Sophia</u>
How long ago was that?

<u>Kylah</u>
About a year ago.

<u>Sophia</u>
Well, this is me judging a book by the cover. You appear to be doing well for yourself. How long would you say it took you to heal and become the successful woman sitting here today?

<u>Kylah</u>
Thank you for saying that. I don't like seeing myself as a victim, even though I know, deep down inside, I will forever be one. That is a label

forever casted upon me. But a few months, close to a year, I decided I wouldn't let that one label define me. I went back to school, but this time I commuted from home, and slowly made new friends. Unfortunately, friendships can fail you too, so after experiencing a backstabbing betrayal, I thought it was best for me to keep my circle small, and that's been working for me for the past few years. It is possible to be happy with just yourself.

<u>Sophia</u>
Have you ruled out romance completely?

<u>Kylah</u>
Yes. By design.

<u>Sophia</u>
Well, before we move on, is there anything else you'd like to share?

<u>Kylah</u>
Yes, actually. To all the ladies listening to my voice, put yourself first. Put your heart second.

Part II.

DEJA

Intermission 4

(Deja taps the back of Kylah's hand)
<u>Deja</u>
You were phenomenal, Kylah.

<u>Sophia</u>
Deja, would you like to share next?

<u>Deja</u>
(She exhales and nods)
I'd be happy to.

<u>Sophia</u>
Great.

<u>Deja</u>
There is one thing.

<u>Sophia</u>
What's that?

<u>Deja</u>
Some news fell in my lap a few days ago, and instead of sharing my story the way Kylah here shared hers, I've prepared something to read. Will that be a problem?

<u>Sophia</u>
I don't see why it would be.

<u>Deja</u>
Thank you.

<u>Sophia</u>
Whenever you're ready, you have the floor. *Hear Me Out*, please welcome Deja Scott.

Chapter 6

Deja

Your funeral will be a huge deal, packed with people from all walks of life. Blue-collar workers, gangsters, thieves, and fast-talking, street-savvy scammers—but most of your mourners will be women.

There will be a competition of thigh-high skirts strutting toward your casket—the mystified, unattached LaMar Wilkins. A parade of women will bounce babies in their arms in front of a grandmother they've never met. She, along with everyone in the church, including your recognized girlfriend, four baby mamas, prying piranhas, and attention-seeking spectators, will wonder who they are, why'd they bring a child to a funeral, and whisper the question: *Are they yours?*

The answer is most likely yes. Yes, another secret child has been conceived that you never gave a second thought. Another innocent being left behind that probably wouldn't have known you anyway, even if your life wasn't cut short.

But *who* really knew you? I sure as hell didn't. I found that out years ago when several rugs were pulled from under me. The old me, who fell for your façade and convincing words you sold me, accompanied by a dark soul that lacked a conscience.

The new me can't help but wonder how you wound up in that wooden box. Did God call you home peacefully, or were you murdered? If it's the latter, will the culprit attend your homegoing service and smile down on you?

You've crossed so many. Which of your crimes finally caught up with you? What con job failed? Who had the gumption to settle the score? What woman you deceived didn't take your disrespect lightly?

Once upon a time, I wanted to cause you harm, make you hurt the way you *made me* hurt, and inflict equal amounts of pain like you imposed upon me.

I told you several times when we were an item how your actions made me hate you. How I'd run you over with a car if I had one and do unspeakable things to you because karma took too long to knock on your door.

But you didn't care. You'd make light of the situation and taunt me with verbal jabs such as, "And that's why you don't have a car," or "I'm gonna give you some time to cool off, Deja."

And we'd do just that. Not talk for days. Then, out of the blue, in the middle of the night, my doorbell would ring.

"Babe, open up. I know you heard me pull up."

I played along. "I thought I needed time to cool off."

"I was just playing when I said that. Babe, don't drag this out. I miss you."

"You should."

"Go put some clothes on. Let's get some breakfast at Waffle House. You know you want a waffle. I'll be out here waiting on you."

I made you sweat, but not enough. I'd throw on something quick and meet you outside. You'd greet me with a kiss and hold me in your arms. We'd laugh like kids amidst drunks and chain smokers while I tore into a waffle and you a patty melt. And just like that, I'd re-enter your maze.

Things between us would be great for a while. You'd surprise me in the stands at my games, shouting my name like a fan, hugging on me like you were proud at the end.

"You did your thing out there, babes." You'd kiss me.

"Thanks for coming."

"No problem. I told you whenever I'm free, I'll be here."

We'd leave the stadium wrapped up in each other's arms, screw like rabbits, bathe, and screw again before you'd leave in the morning. And the cycle would repeat.

You must have gotten a kick out of your stellar performance—

lying to my face, knowing you were going to continue treating me like the dummy I unwillingly signed up to play in your production. Because the familiar pattern would resurface, and you'd have me

waiting for you. And waiting for you. We'd miss events because you'd arrive to pick me up hours late, or not at all, and I'd have to write you off again.

Dating you became a constant state of make-up to break-up. Of me smiling then crying, and you breaking promises and lying. Eventually working yourself back inside of me.

I remember that delusional girl hanging onto your every word. Every lie. The used-to-be-smart girl who got good grades with daddy issues. The bright-eyed girl longing for someone to love and have them love her back.

But you turned me into the stupid girl living with delusions of grandeur. An unwise girl who thought that we were an item. A real dumb-dumb that got a kick out at how girls faces would drop when they saw us together.

When rumors of you whoring around the city came into question, you convinced me they weren't true.

"Those guys are saying that because they hate me. They just want to sleep with you," you said.

I laugh now when I reflect on how my brain stopped working the year I was tied to you.

I asked God for forgiveness when I told my sister you passed away. She and I laughed briefly and apologized with our heads tilted to the sky. It was disrespectful of us yet surprising we both had the same reaction.

She asked me, "Foul play?"

I replied, "I was wondering the same thing."

And then we laughed out loud for at least five seconds before pulling ourselves together.

That was crass of us, but your history, and the horrible way you treated me, had to be the reason she and I shared the same sentiment.

Once we settled down, she asked, "What made you deal with him for so long?"

Chapter 7

DEJA

I was tongue-tied, trying to answer her question. Sure, you complimented me and made me feel special by flattering me with sweet words and gestures.

"You're so pretty, babe," you'd tell me, and put my feet in your lap and say, "Tell your man how your day was," while gazing into my eyes and glossing over me like I was who you desired.

Your brown eyes had power in them. They'd make my chest pound like drums in a marching band. And when you talked to me during our passionate moments, you had a way of showing dominance while simultaneously praising me—a first for clueless, punch-drunk-in-love me.

I blushed from embarrassment that the answer to my sister's question was sex. How ridiculous of me to be consumed by a man-boy that spoke fabricated lies with ease and contributed to the birth of a gazillion children. A man with an uncertain future had *me*, co-captain of the San Diego Soccer Stars, wrapped around his finger.

Why? Because you were the most handsome man I had ever laid eyes on. I was hard up for your smooth, cocoa skin, full lips, almond eyes, and firm chest.

My inexperience thought you were a life-changing lay when we wrinkled the sheets. In my eyes, you were the total package. But in reality, you were a disappointment filled with lies pumping through your veins. The perfect recipe for a young girl unwise to the wickedness in the world.

My silence from the question was followed by a memory my sister never put to bed.

"Remember that time he had you so messed up I had to come and pick you up because you couldn't stop crying? Then, after a week, you begged me to take you back home so he could stomp all over your soft heart again?"

"Yeah. I remember. I call that the dumb age."

"I probably shouldn't agree with you, but you were for that douche. We all were at some point for the wrong guy. Thank goodness you snapped out of it, and may he rest in peace."

We ended the call as flashes of our past nearly sent me in a tizzy. The humiliation and degradation you inflicted on me resurfaced, and the hatred I felt toward myself back then stung my chest.

I remembered the first time we met, when I gave you a fake number. My spirit said to send you away, and I listened. Our paths crossed a second time, and you stole the spotlight from another guy keeping me company at homecoming. You refused to let me give him another second of my time, and I wound up giving it to you because of your persistence. I didn't think giving you the correct number that time would be one of my biggest regrets.

Your powers of persuasion convinced me to let down my wall, and give myself to you, only to be rewarded with a sharp dagger to my chest. The buried resentment I felt for you reminded me to never be that stupid again. The moment your mind games made me question my sanity was the moment I should have walked away. Unfortunately, my young mind was no match for your gift of gaslighting. And on top of that, you turned out to be a thief.

You stole from me, physically and mentally. You were like a magician with your five-finger discount. A smooth kleptomaniac that would steal my property. I wouldn't notice what was missing for weeks. But being the great liar that you were, you'd sell me a story that I forced myself to believe with willful ignorance when, deep down, I knew you were lying to my face. It came naturally to you—just like seeing the best in people came naturally to me. Shame on me for that.

Shame on you for taking advantage of me because I lacked boundaries. You'd lie and say you had a business trip out of town. For days, you'd be gone, checking in with me at night via text or a call. Imagine my surprise when my teammate shared that you were seen at the unit next to hers around the corner from where I live.

The bullet wound didn't end there, though. The apartment belonged to your daughter's mother, who was pregnant with your baby, which you denied.

"Your friend must have seen someone over there that looked like me. My ex is cool people. I told you that. We have a good co-parenting relationship. That's all."

Had I known the real you, that would have been the end of us. But you wouldn't let me off that easy. You continued to hurt me to my core, showed me you could be worse, and took me past hell. Damn near flambéed me like I was cherries jubilee and tested how far you could lower my respect. The answer: to the gutter.

Horrible rumors surfaced about your involvement with girls at one of the high schools: a cheerleader, a girl in the choir, a pass around—the list was never-ending.

One of your friends confirmed the rumors and

told me everything I needed to know. I was sick to my stomach when the real portrait of you was painted for me to see with broad strokes. I begged you to leave me alone, cursed you out, and blocked your calls. I made it clear we were done and slowly regained my peace. I was free from your web.

I re-entered the dating pool. You found out and wouldn't leave me be.

"I need to see you," you said.

"I'm at work. Don't call me here."

"We need to talk. What time do you get off tonight?"

"Eight. Why?"

"I'll pick you up out front. See you in a few. You hear me?"

I agreed to see you one final time. That was the defining moment I deserved the *dumbest girl in the world* award. You, the man in the hot seat, the man on the chopping block, didn't have the decency to be early or on time for a meeting *you* requested.

But there I was, waiting on you—yet again—outside of the hotel where *I* was in training for a night-management position.

Frigid winds blew over and around me as guests checked in and out for more than an hour. And I was afraid you would drive off if I wasn't standing out front when you arrived, so I froze my ass off in the freezing cold.

Fuming, calling you like a maniac, and incessantly checking the time on my phone, I could feel the hatred burning through me like a furnace. To add insult to injury, my manager, John, pulled his car up to me at the entrance of the hotel just as you turned into the parking lot.

"I've been looking at you from my office, wondering why you are standing out here. It's freezing. I can't stand to watch this anymore. Hop in," he said.

I happily accepted his offer, wiggling my toes in my heels to get my blood flowing.

John's eyes widened. "Oh. I thought you were out here just suffering in the cold. I couldn't tell you were down here crying from my vantage point. What's going on? Is everything okay?"

I nodded and sniffled, looking at your silhouette behind the tinted windows.

"You live downtown, right?" John confirmed.

"Yes, sir," I mumbled, studying the glimmer of light shining against your face.

John's eyes followed mine. "Is that who you were waiting for?"

"Yes." My hand reached for the handle of the door.

"Please don't do that. Anyone who left you standing out here in the cold doesn't care about you." He put the car in drive, hit the gas, and sped off.

"I know he doesn't."

"I'd be livid if some fuckboy was treating my sister the way that guy is obviously treating you. You need to choose better."

"I know. I did. I broke up with him, and he begged to pick me up after work to hear him out. I canceled my ride home like an idiot to hear what he had to say." I lifted my hand. "I know that was a mistake."

You flashed your lights as we approached the edge of the lot.

John sighed. "Is this guy going to be a problem?"

I shrugged, wiping away the tears salting my cheeks.

Then, you called my phone. "Whose car did you get in?"

"My manager."

"Tell him to pull over!" you yelled at me like I was your child.

"No. Just go home."

"You better get out of that fuckin' car! If you don't, when we get to your house, I'm gonna spit on you, and then I'm gonna beat his ass!"

John instructed me to end the call. I keeled over with the phone pressed to my chest as you continued to shout obscenities like a madman while tailgating us onto the highway.

I hung up on you.

"Call the police," said John. "Request that a car be stationed outside of your house."

The tone of his voice would not settle for me to say no, so I relayed my address to the operator while I ignored your back-to-back calls on the other line. Funny how our roles reversed because you weren't getting your way.

As John parked, he lectured me like he was my big brother and not my boss. He apologized *for your* actions, while pitying me like a fragile bird lost without its mother.

His kindness extended into words of affirmation, and he promised to keep my drama between the two of us. Most of all, he showed me how a real man should treat a woman. Not just a woman in distress, but a woman who needed assurance that not all men were like you.

Then, you parked behind his car like an obsessed, jilted boyfriend, as if you had the right after all you had done to me.

John's face turned pasty white with sorrow as he listened to my sob story. Your continuous calls had to be silenced while I bared my soul to him about what I tolerated from you. He pitied me by the time I was done, which was when the blue lights appeared in the distance, then you sped off in the opposite direction.

My manager explained to the officer that he was

concerned for my safety. I was grateful he protected me from a domestic dispute.

The officer asked if I wanted to file a report, but I declined. Was it because I loved or suddenly feared you, I wondered. That answer never became clear, but with certainty, I knew I would never welcome you back into my house.

I returned to work the next day, slid a thank-you note under my manager's door, and gave my notice. My sister and her fiancée helped me move a week later, and I breathed comfortably as I fled the city limits, happy to no longer share the same air as you.

Did I think about you? Yes. On dates. At parties. In the shower. While getting my hair chopped off. But don't flatter yourself. Time served as my healer for the hell you put me through. Also, a message I received from one of your friends. The same friend that snitched about your dealings behind my back.

Months after I moved away, he sent word through one of our mutuals.

"Tell Deja I wish she could have seen LaMar's face the other night. He was bragging that none of us had a loyal girl like him the other night. He said, "I can pull up to my girl's house any time of the night, and there will never be another man warming my side of the bed." He had no idea she moved, and when we pointed out her apartment was dark and hollow and there wasn't any furniture inside, he looked scrambled."

What I would have given to see you humbled. To see your beautiful face realize you no longer had power over me. To see you feel a smidgen of how I felt wasting my precious time, thoughts, body, and energy on the likes of you.

Your torment and sadistic ways taught me a valuable lesson—to never put a man before myself. To understand that men like you wake up searching for naïve women like I was. That there is evil in the most innocent spaces, and good looks often mask a devil in the flesh.

A friend I hadn't heard from in a while called me when the news broke about your passing. She asked if I had heard the news, then stunned me when I told her I had.

"Sorry for your loss," she said.

To me.

Mystified by her choice of words, my face crumpled. "What do you mean 'sorry for your loss'? I'm happily married and left that drama behind me years ago. I'm sorry he's dead, but I have no loss."

Other than being confused about what kind of friend would call me and say such nonsense, I had an epiphany. I had gotten over you without realizing it. I didn't hate you anymore, hadn't thought about you in years. And that puzzled me.

Not remembering when you were truly out of my system made me smile. *When did that happen?* I wondered. Where was my sense of urgency to cry at sad news? What happened to my compassion?

I won't give it much thought, for dwelling on our tumultuous past can't be undone, but it taught me many lessons. And that was to learn from my mistakes, raise my standards, and never settle.

Removing you from my life led me to the happiness I deserved. More importantly, love. The good kind that doesn't make you cry.

Intermission 5

<u>Sophia</u>
Deja. The look on your face. It's different from when you began reading.

<u>Deja</u>
Is it?

<u>Sophia</u>
You look at peace. Softer.

<u>Deja</u>
Do I? I thought you were gonna say I look flushed. I feel kind of embarrassed, but if my story helps someone else, then it was worth sharing.

<u>Sophia</u>

Why do you feel embarrassed?

Deja
Because I let a man drag me. I had to have been out of my mind. Ugh. I started not to show up today.

Sophia
Well, we're glad you did show up.

Deja
Thank you. Writing this was kind of triggering. I must admit, I omitted a few things that were too hard to relive. Tsk, tsk, tsk. If only I had known then what I know now. Unfortunately, the world doesn't work that way.

Sophia
If I may ask, are you still in contact with the manager that took you home?

Deja
When I left, I was determined to leave everything behind me. Him. That job. The friends we had in common. All of it. I'd probably tell him thank you if our paths were to ever cross again. Though, I thanked him a million times before I quit my job.

<u>Sophia</u>

I am curious... Did your ex really pass away, or was what you read a creative outlet?

<u>Deja</u>

Oh no, he's really dead.

<u>Sophia</u>

How does his death make you feel?

<u>Deja</u>

Like I said in my letter, I was surprised the news of it didn't affect me. Normally, something like that would. But I meant every word of what I said. And before the righteous seek me out with their teachings about forgiveness and all that religious rhetoric that I believe is 100% contradictory, save it. I think forgiveness is overrated—or at least the way I view it. I don't fully believe in the concept. I've heard forgiveness is for yourself, and I don't buy it. I forgive by forgetting. And what I learned from that relationship was I had to stop looking at people as good and kind. There are only a handful of people in this world that can be considered good. And I used to be one of them, but I'm not as soft anymore.

Sophia

There's a lot to unpack there, but let's end on a positive note. You mentioned happiness at the end of your letter. Are you...happy?

Deja

Very much so. Happily married to an amazing man.

Sophia

Fantastic. It's good to hear you didn't give up on love.

Deja

Turns out my mother use to give me solid advice when it comes to men. If you have to wonder if he loves you, then he doesn't. Actions speak louder than words, and I found one that showed me how he felt about me. It feels amazing not having to guess.

Part III.

MONA LISA

Intermission 6

<u>Mona Lisa</u>
At least you were able to trust someone again. I don't think I'll ever be able to do that again.

<u>Deja</u>
I won't argue with you. It's a miracle I was able to.

<u>Sophia</u>
I hear you both. But do you think that's fair to yourselves? What I mean is, do you think a person can miss out on something great by allowing what someone else did to you in the past dictate your future?

<u>Mona Lisa</u>
I can't speak for the others, but as for me, no.

Every time I have wiped the slate clean, it's the same outcome. I mean, men are out here blaming women for picking wrong. How about you tell your fuckboy friend to not do wrong things. Not lie to women. String them along. Use them as placeholders while blocking them from this mythical "supposed" good guy that could be waiting around the corner. Ya know?

<u>Sophia</u>
Sounds like you have quite a story to tell. If you're ready...

<u>Mona Lisa</u>
I am.

<u>Sophia</u>
Everyone, Mona Lisa Whitmore.

CHAPTER 8

MONA LISA

Men have been horrible to me, and I've wrestled with that being my fault because I picked the wrong guys to date let men tell it. They say *pick better*. So, I did. I went from dating old friends and whorish athletes, to dating the smart guy with a nine-to-five, the ugly guy, and average-Joe hardworking man. They all shared the same agenda: hit it and quit it, shuffle me around on their playboy board, hide their real lives, and waste my time.

I was too young to settle down when I dated the average Joe, the kind people say girls should give a chance because they are known to be good men. Lesson one: people don't know what the hell they are talking about. That man nearly broke my soul when he showed me that he did not like me.

And all he had to do was tell me that. Instead, he used me like the rest of the dirtbags I believed before him. But what hurt the most was how he damaged me.

My average Joe was the friend of my good friend, Vincent, who referred me to my first decent paying job after college. I must have wreaked of youth and stupidity when he sought me out. Me simply doing a friend a favor, by taking him home after work and accepting to eat breakfast that his roommate cooked, turned into an all-day affair. Innocent at first.

We exchanged information, and that was all she wrote. The next time I drove my good friend home, I didn't eat and run. I stayed. All day.

The night ended with an extensive roll in the hay —one that had me smiling when I crept out early in the morning to go home and shower before my shift.

When I clocked in, Vincent joked, "You good, Mo?"

"Yeah. Why do you ask?"

"You look a little tired."

"Long night."

We laughed.

"You surprised me, girl."

"I surprised myself. Your friend moves quick. I think I really like him."

The silent response of Vincent's raised eyebrows told me what I needed to know. I paid attention to the warning and played it coy until he reached out to me.

In my mind, I was doing everything the ominous "they" tell you to do when it comes to dating. "They" say it's best to date a friend of a friend. Check. "They" also say don't chase the man; let him chase you. Check.

After a few weeks and several long adventurous nights, I noticed the change. The calls weren't as frequent, and the late nights turned into short stops at my place. Quickies with no cuddling. Lame excuses that I pretended didn't piss me off. I was now doing another thing "they" say to do—don't nag your man or let him see you mad.

Where I screwed up was thinking my average Joe was my man. He acted like it in the beginning, but within a few months, he displayed the same pattern as the others. And I still kept myself available for when he called, which was only one more time.

His eyes looked weird the next time I saw him. He stared at me as if he was holding something back.

"What's that look for?"

"What look?" he lied.

"The one on your face, like you have something you wanna say. If you don't like me anymore, just tell me. I won't wild out on you."

"You trippin'."

"Am I? We've been seeing less and less of each other."

"'Cause of my overtime. We're short-staffed right now."

"So you've said. Well, whatever it is you aren't telling me, I can wait for when you're ready."

He spent the night at my place that night. He left at the first sight of light sneaking through the shades, and I came up with the most ridiculous idea ever. I surprised him at work with fast food for lunch, since he claimed they were so busy with overtime.

The receptionist showed me to the visitor's lounge, but I didn't sit because I had to get back to work myself. The lounge had wide-open glass around it for visitors to see the first row of operations in the plant. People smiled at me as they walked by—the opposite of what my average Joe did when he saw it was me standing in the lounge.

The glass mirrored a reflection of him against the window of an office opposite the lounge.

"Fuck," he mouthed when he saw me, then entered the room unaware I saw his reaction in the glass.

My heart raced with pain, bouncing like Roy Jones punching a speed bag. I didn't love this man. I liked him, but not enough to give him the power to make me feel so small, and cut me down like a withering tree ruining the neighborhood. No. I was being nice and regretted having a kind heart in that moment. So when he walked into the room, I pretended I didn't see what he said.

I plastered on a dim smile. "Sorry to bother you. You said you were busy with overtime, and I was on my way to an appointment. I thought I'd bring you lunch." I handed him the bag. "I've got to get going so I won't be late. Have a good rest of your day." I wiggled my fingers and walked out.

"Thank you," he said, in a stumped, modest tone, I assumed because he thought I was going to fawn over him.

We didn't talk after that, but he wasn't out of my life completely. Weeks later, I figured out what he wasn't saying the last time we slept together when a persistent cough rattled in my chest. Over-the-counter meds didn't work. Herbal teas were a waste of time. And three weeks of hacking up my lungs required a visit to the doctor.

When the M.D. couldn't find anything wrong, she suggested I see an OBGYN. The fear of those letters damn near gave me a heart attack.

"What for? I just had my period. I'm not pregnant."

"I fear you may have an STI."

"You think that from a cough?"

She sat down in her rolling chair, eased up to her computer, typed her doctor codes, then turned her screen toward me.

"You're young, Mona Lisa. You're always nice when you come in for a visit. I feel compelled to tell you to be careful out here. If you don't have an OBGYN, I can refer you to a friend. If he has an opening, can you make time to see him today?"

"You sound so serious."

"Because your health is serious. One mistake can mess up the rest of your life. Wait here. Let me make a call."

Waiting for her to return to the room with my appointment was nothing like waiting for the culture results at her colleague's office. But I was grateful she cared enough about me as a patient to find me the cure for my cough.

My insensitive average Joe had given me an STI, like she suspected, which led to my first HIV test. The other tests didn't compare to the wait time for that one. When this took place, you had to wait three days to find out the fate of your life, but by His grace and mercy, the results were negative.

I was told to reach out to the perpetrator passing penis poison around. But I didn't call him. I wouldn't give him the satisfaction of seeing my number on his ignored call list for further humiliation. He knew what he was carrying that last night he slept in my bed, and I learned that fun sometimes came with a loan and compounding interest that could have cost me for a lifetime. I should have killed him.

INTERMISSION 7

<u>Sophia</u>
Mona Lisa, what that man did to you was
absolutely horrific.

<u>Mona Lisa</u>
Yes it was. I hope I inspire a young woman out
there to be ten times more careful.

<u>Sophia</u>
Earlier, I asked Kylah and Deja a few
uncomfortable questions. I have a few for you if
you don't mind my asking.

<u>Mona Lisa</u>
That's fair.

<u>Sophia</u>

Is there a reason you refer to this man as average
Joe and not his real name?

Mona Lisa
Because that's how I will always think of him.
Average.

Sophia
Are you still friends with the friend that
introduced you to him?

Mona Lisa
No. He was one of those friends that come in
your life for a season and a reason.

Sophia
Have you seen or heard from this average Joe
since you walked away from him?

Mona Lisa
Actually, I did run into him. Several years later,
I was out with a group of women and he
happened to be at the same bar. His eyes damn
near penetrated my skin, but I'm great at
ignoring people and continued to enjoy my
night. I guess, in his mind, he thought he had
the rizz to run game on me like he did back in
the day. A waitress came to our table with

drinks and pointed at him sitting with a proud grin on his face. "That gentleman sent you ladies these drinks." We all looked his way, and he raised his glass. I smiled and waved at him, then told the waitress to give the drinks to three ladies standing around waiting for a table to open up. "Tell them we're about to leave, and they can have our booth." The women came over, we exchanged pleasantries, and my friends and I gave up our seats. I warned the ladies. "If a tall guy wearing an auburn-colored jacket and matching shirt hits on any of you tonight, run for the hills. He has a dirty dick. Do not pass go. Y'all be safe tonight.

Sophia

What was his reaction to you giving away the drinks?

Mona Lisa

I wouldn't know. I went on about my business.

Sophia

What you went through was repulsive, but you got your power back in the end.

Mona Lisa

Perhaps. I'm more proud that I didn't give him

the reaction he wanted. It felt good not to give a damn.

Sophia
Good for you.

Mona Lisa
Things *are* good for me now, but back then, trouble found me again the following year unfortunately. And I had to make some serious life changes after meeting a man named Dwight.

CHAPTER 9

MONA LISA

Dwight, no last name—because he lied to me about it. A name I have never mentioned to anyone. Ever. Until now.

After the scare with my average Joe, I didn't date. I thought reading self-help books and cutting myself off from the web of the world's worst men would give me better clarity in my decision making. In short, it did not.

I grew lonely. And with loneliness comes a need for affection. Attention. Touch.

A rule I swear by is—*never look back once you're ahead*. I don't circle the block or give second chances when relationships don't work out. They didn't work out for a reason, and I don't take interest in experiencing second rounds of punishment.

After the big scare, I thought a new beginning was in order. I moved out of my apartment into a house with the option to buy closer to the city limits. I had zero intention of buying it, but it was afford-able with a third roommate, and it allowed me the peace of new walls that paint could not bring.

Being in a new space, with new décor, and the new year approaching infused a good energy around me. I thought it was time to put myself out there and dip my toes back into the sea, hoping to land a fish.

My roomies and I had plans to party hop on New Year's Eve, but one fell sick, and the other bailed at the last minute to cover a coworker's shift and earn some extra cash.

I was dolled up with a fresh silk press, cute black dress and heels, and a list of parties to crash solo, but I never made it to one. Instead, I fell victim to a smooth talker in the parking lot of the A&P.

I made a last minute stop for a few cheap bottles of wine to pass on to the hosts of each party I was going to attend. A set of light-brown eyes followed me down the aisle as I searched for a deal on Pinot and Chianti. Those same eyes checked out before me in the line and waited for me at the entrance.

He asked, "Do you need help carrying those bags?"

"I got it," I said, returning his smile.

"Where are you going with all that wine?"

"House parties."

"Can I come?"

"Sorry. It's invite-only."

"Damn. Wish I was there to get my New Year's kiss at midnight."

"From who?"

"From you. That's all I could think about when I saw you in there."

"And how do you know I don't already have someone to kiss at midnight?"

"Because if you were my girl, you wouldn't be out here by yourself this time of night. Fuck those parties. Bring the year in with me."

"I don't know you."

"Get to know me." He extended his hand. "Dwight Shepard."

"Mona Lisa."

"You're way prettier than that painting, Mona Lisa."

"So I've been told."

"Well it's true. So how about it? You wanna bring this new year in with me?"

And I did.

It was nice. I followed him back to his place, getting lost with all the twists and turns in a new subdivision in Decatur. The homes appeared to be two to three thousand square feet, if not bigger, and the neighborhood was impressive—gate protected, beautifully manicured with pole lights around the clubhouse, and green lawns for half a mile to play miniature golf.

Dwight lived in a yellow, two-story house fresh off the market in the back of the neighborhood. I parked my car behind his in the driveway, and he stood outside my door and opened it for me.

Such a gentleman, I thought, taking his hand as he pressed the button of a control to open the garage.

Exercise equipment, a dinette set, and half-opened boxes filled the parking spaces like a storage unit when the doors lifted. Once I was inside, it was clear he had just moved in, and that sparked our conversation.

"Did you have help moving in, or did you hire a service?"

"Movers brought everything inside, but I have more to do to piece this place fully together."

"Where are you moving from?"

"Up top," he said.

I detected the New York accent, so I asked, "What borough are you from?"

"The Bronx." He grinned. "What you know about the boroughs?"

"I travel and have friends across the country. You seemed shocked."

"Not shocked. Just checking you out. What would you like to drink?"

"I don't drink."

His brows furrowed. "I just met you buying wine."

"For my hosts." I laughed. "Did you think I was some sort of lush?"

"No. But if you were, you'd be the prettiest lush by far."

His flattery made me nervous. Especially because it was working. I shifted the conversation.

"Can I look around?"

"Be my guest."

I broke free from him. I had to. I already knew I was going to sleep with him when I agreed to go to his place. Like I said earlier, I was lonely. It had been a year since I felt the touch of a man or felt stirrings flow through me from conversation. And he was saying all the right things and looking at me like he was going to deliver everything I was missing.

He allowed me to snoop on my own. I opened drawers, searched the bathroom cabinet for female items, and brushed through the clothes hanging in the closet of the master bedroom.

Dwight surprised me from behind. "Find *whatcha* looking for?"

"I did. I like a man who dresses well and has a sense of organization. Chaos is my kryptonite."

He grabbed me by the hand. "Come on. I have the television on in the living room. The ball is about to drop."

"Sounds like someone is missing home."

"I would if you weren't here right now."

The ball dropped, and so did his pants when the kiss at midnight never ended. He carried me into the master bedroom like in the scene from *An Officer & a Gentleman*, and I was so far gone and caught up in the moment, that when the latex joined the party, I was just as ready as him to proceed.

It was how I imagined it would be. Hot and heavy with a hint of magic sprinkled in each stroke.

His groans boosted my ego, assuring me that I hadn't lost my rhythm. And when the pleasure my access gave to him came to an end, there was no awkwardness. We talked like we were old friends until we fell asleep, and he held me all night while I slept below his buff arms like I was in my own bed.

I woke up before him. The sun was bright in the room since the drapes were still inside a bag on the floor next to the rods. I studied Dwight up close, learning his features in the daylight, wondering what he was dreaming as his eyes flinched behind his closed lids.

He woke up and caught me staring at him. We didn't speak. He smiled at me and pulled me closer then caressed my face before kissing me.

I covered my mouth. "Good morning. I should get going so I can brush my teeth and take a bath, so I don't have bad breath and soiled skin all year."

"I didn't take you to be superstitious."

"Superstitious or not, I worship cleanliness."

"But I'm not ready for you to leave."

"I can come back with a toiletry bag."

He rolled on top of me. "Well, you can't leave without giving me a proper goodbye." He slipped his tongue in my mouth and rubbed his erection against my leg. "I haven't had enough of you, Lisa."

"What's my full name?"

"Mona Lisa." He hunched on me. "Trust me. Your name has stained my tongue."

That tongue he spoke of tasted me until I called out his name.

"That's what I wanted to hear," he said. "You ready for me?"

I nodded. "Yes. Do you have another condom?"

He reached into the drawer of the nightstand and suited up. When he first penetrated, his moans sounded the same as they did hours before, but as we got further into it, he became more vocal. Praising how good I felt. Groaning with more intensity. And stroking me vigorously this time as if he was trying to leave a lasting impression to make me keep my word and return with an overnight bag.

This session lasted longer than the first one. And I had zero complaints or concern until he began to growl, which took me out of the moment. I looked up at his closed eyes as his teeth sank into his bottom lip, when something cold and sticky tapped on my cheek.

"Goddamn, girl." He sighed. "Mona, Mona, Mona." He groaned. "Lisa," he whispered. "I was right about you."

The sticky object stuck to my ass cheek, so I leaned up and peeked between our bodies between his thrusts. Suddenly, Dwight clung to my hips and shivered on top of me, while I, on the other hand, grew filled with rage trying to free myself.

His body trembled more than the first time he relieved himself. And his verbal exertions were louder with a mixture of low growls, grunts, and groans.

When his quavering began to subside, I managed to shove him off of me.

"Why did you do that!" I yelled at him, jumping up from the bed.

His friendly grin now looked sinister.

"I had to feel you for real. And I was right. You got that fire."

I redressed quickly like stage performers between scenes. He threw on his boxers and ran behind me as I fled down the stairs.

"Why are you running away? Talk to me."

I grabbed my keys and purse from the sofa in the living room, holding back my tears. I couldn't give him the satisfaction of seeing me cry, giving away the power I had just reclaimed, and ruining the new year I had so much hope for.

He gripped my waist. "Chill, baby. *We got* all day to sort this out. Let me put on some clothes, and we'll go grab a bite and talk about it."

I sat down to get him out of my face.

He went into the kitchen and grabbed a beer from the fridge, then slid a bottle of water on the coffee table in front of me. "I'll be right back."

I stared at his back as he made his way up the stairs. When the coast was clear, I searched the house for a piece of mail to make a record of his address, but came up empty. As a last resort, I scurried into the kitchen and found a bill under a magnet on the fridge. The tears I was holding back dropped at the sight of the last name on the power bill, which differed from what he told me. He said his name was Dwight Shepard. The bill read Dwight Simmons.

I was confused at why he would do that. He brought me to his new house. Why lie and show me where you live and lie about your surname? Who the hell did I sleep with? And what the fuck was wrong with me?

I stuffed the envelope in my purse but didn't press the issue, as I was more concerned with the picture of the exotic woman with long, black, silky hair on the magnet.

I yelled from the bottom of the stairs. "Dwight!"

"Yeah, baby!"

"Who is the woman on the fridge?"

The silhouette of his shadow came into the light, rising from the bottom of the wall at the top of the stairs.

"That's my wife, but let me explain."

I bolted to the front door. It was locked with a dead bolt, and the key was missing. Dwight ran into me on my way back to the living room.

"I'm separated. She didn't want to move down south, and I got a good job offer down here, so we split up. That's the honest truth."

To me, that translated as he was getting the house set up before she arrived, and I was the easiest piece of ass he could score, so he would string me along until she moved into their new home. Finally, my brain cells activated.

"Open the garage, please."

"Mona, Mona, I swear I ain't lying."

"Just like you weren't lying when you shed that condom and exposed me. Open the garage. I won't ask you again."

He took his slow-ass time to get the remote.

"Hurry up before I start breaking shit!"

Miraculously, the door lifted. He followed me outside, saying words, but I heard nothing. I left tire marks in his driveway and drove home with a new-found hatred for men and a secret I thought I would take to the grave.

It wasn't until I saw an episode of Michaela Coel's *I May Destroy You*, that what Dwight did to me is considered rape. I had no idea that removing contraception qualified as sexual assault.

In having that knowledge now, and looking back at what transpired back then, I don't think I would have filed charges against him, because I went home with a stranger. I consented to sleep with him after a matter of minutes, and I was a fool for falling for his game. I felt guilty and still feel guilty for making bad decisions, even though I've learned I was not at fault.

That New Year's was the worst of my life, and Dwight Lying Ass Last Name was the worst person I've ever met. He turned me into an ignorant adulteress, love-seeking simpleton, that eventually transformed me into Lady Stone Heart.

I was groomed to not give a fuck because of the company I chose to keep. I lost myself looking for something in others, and that has been the hardest fact I've had to work on for my mental health.

Having to be tested for a second round of STI exams robbed me of a world filled with color. Everything turned gray. Even when I was told I was in the clear, life felt dull and tasteless.

And though this happened many moons ago, the bitterness sneaks up on me when I least expect it.

When I'm at weddings, I put on airs, no longer seeing it as a beautiful reward or treasured union. Dwight took that from me. He erased the idea of marriage, and love, and the belief that everyone has a soulmate with predestined ties. He confirmed that some of us have been given the fate of darkness, no matter how much they dream or obey the rules, and forced me to accept the answer was in front of me all along when I look at the lives of our mothers, grandmothers, and their mothers before them.

To be happy in this world, love is not and never has been enough. And to be told you're pretty by a man means absolutely nothing.

Intermission 8

<u>Sophia</u>
Mona Lisa, I believe every word you've said, but
I am speechless.

<u>Mona Lisa</u>
So was I, for a while. Do you have any questions
for me?

<u>Sophia</u>
I do. Did you think about confronting this man
when you found out that what he did is
considered assault?

<u>Mona Lisa</u>
I thought about doing more than confronting
him, so I talked myself out of doing anything
at all.

Sophia

Are you a little bit curious if his wife ever found out what kind of man she married?

Mona Lisa

For a short while I wondered if she knew, but I could never be the person to turn another woman's world upside down.

Sophia

That's understandable. Like the others, you appear to be getting on fine. How did you do it?

Mona Lisa

It took me years to want to be touched by another man. That caused a few problems with men—several failed relationships, to be honest.

Sophia

Because you didn't want to get physical?

Mona Lisa

Precisely. I had the urges but couldn't act on them. I had trouble trusting anyone for a long time, but when I raised my standards and forgave myself for my past mistakes, my discernment got stronger.

<u>Sophia</u>
But you said you stopped believing in love.

<u>Mona Lisa</u>
I have. I don't understand it, therefore I stopped believing in it. I can't say that it doesn't exist. I just know it doesn't exist for me, which is why I'm a serial dater. I don't want to be attached to any other living soul, and I enjoy living day to day free from what's considered the social norm.

<u>Sophia</u>
What would be the one thing that needs to happen to change your mind?

(Mona Lisa smiles)
<u>Mona Lisa</u>
A woman president.

<u>Sophia</u>
And we'll be back after this short break.

Part IV.

SOPHIA

Intermission 9

<u>Sophia</u>

Today, we've heard some heavy testimony from our guests. Mona Lisa, Deja, and Kylah have given us inspiration to battle demons when misfortune drives them our way. Before we say good night, I wanted to share an observation. I noticed you ladies refrained from using the word love. Not one of you confessed to loving the men that violated you. Would any of you like to weigh in on why that is?

<u>Mona Lisa</u>

I liked the two men that stomped all over me. I didn't spend enough time with either one of them long enough to love them.

<u>Deja</u>

I thought I was in love with LaMar. When you're young, you tend to use that word too early and have no idea what it means. Now that I'm older, I think what I was feeling was a combination of lust, infatuation, and shallow attraction. My confusion caused me to put up with the horrible way he treated me because I didn't love myself. I think a lot of young girls experience that.

<u>Sophia</u>
Experience not loving themselves?

<u>Deja</u>
Exactly. Hormones affect us in so many different ways. One of the reasons I wanted to tell my story is because this new age of people sharing their stories online has shown me that a lot— and I mean a lot—of women regret the men they chose to love. And I think it's because we don't really love ourselves at that stage. We fall for seductive words and big gestures because we are searching for the love we're missing inside. When I compare how I felt back then versus now, I would not have tolerated a man berating me like that.

<u>Sophia</u>

What about you, Kylah?

<u>Kylah</u>
That man's name and love don't belong in the same sentence. I was young, desperate, and lost. Not in love. We never uttered those words to each other. Love couldn't exist with such a person. Hate did. And it still does.

<u>Sophia</u>
Have any of your exes tried to contact you?

<u>Deja</u>
Before LaMar died?...not that I'm aware.

<u>Mona Lisa</u>
If what they say is true about The Book of Faces app, the average Joe's profile pops up on my recommend list quite often. "They" say that happens when someone searches for you or views your page. I got tired of seeing his stupid face, so I hit the block button.

<u>Sophia</u>
Kylah?

<u>Kylah</u>
The day he does is the day he dies.

<u>Sophia</u>

Okay. Any final words you want to share with the audience?

<u>Kylah</u>

A few. If you have to lie, he isn't worth it. Know that a man will tell you what you want to hear. Make him show you what you want. Never give a man money. File a report when you are violated. Fuck your pride. It comes before the fall. Marriage isn't for everyone. And there is nothing wrong with being a cat lady.

<u>Sophia</u>

Mona Lisa?

<u>Mona Lisa</u>

Watch your thoughts; they become your words. Watch your words; they become your actions. Always run a background check and require that your partner take a test upfront. Trust is earned and should never be given easily. And be careful who you greet with a smile. They don't always hold the best intentions.

<u>Sophia</u>

And Deja?

Deja

Don't stay in a toxic relationship. It'll never be worth it. Trust your gut, and love yourself before you love anyone else. A small few get their happy ending. Believe that is what's in store for you.

Sophia

To our audience, today's content was brought to you to spread awareness about abuse. It can be mental, physical, verbal, emotional, financial, or sexual. If you are in need of help, contact Violence Against Women. You don't have to suffer, and you are not alone. I'm Sophia Mally, asking that you *Hear Me Out.*

CHAPTER 10

SOPHIA

"Ladies, if there is anything you ever need, please let me know," I say to the courageous three before they leave the studio.

Sean escorts the women out of the building while I secure the files on a back-up drive. She returns and throws the empty water bottles in the recycle bin, polishes the wood until the fingerprints are removed from the round table, and lowers the lights.

"Congrats on another great show."

I shrug. "Hopefully the trauma and lessons our guests have shared will reach and teach the younger generation of women to make better choices."

"That is the point, after all. Will the episode be ready to air on Monday?"

"I will edit what I can tonight and finish in the morning, so we should air on schedule. Did you get what we needed from the interview?"

"Mostly."

"Good. Bring what you find back here in the morning, and I'll do the same."

"Sure thing. Now, can you explain why…"

I shake my head side to side. "Grab your jacket and meet me out front."

Sean locks the door, zipping her jacket as she approaches me standing on the sidewalk. I give her a stern look. She reads it then follows my lead of bogus conversation along our walk to the ice cream shop a few blocks from the studio.

I place our usual order, cold brew cookie dough on a waffle cone and peanut butter fudge tracks. We exit the parlor.

"There's a dead man in the backseat of my car," I say behind my cone.

"Who?" she asks with the spoon in her mouth.

"I haven't a clue. He was hiding in the backseat of my car. I can only assume I was his intended target. I saw his silhouette when the sun beamed through the tint. So, when I went to get into my car, I stunned him with my taser a couple of times. I asked him a round of questions. "Who are you? Who sent you? Why are you in my car?" Instead of answering, he charged at me, so I tased him one more time and stabbed him to death. He should have answered my questions. I would have spared him—maybe."

Sean never asks many questions. Without further

explanation, she plops in the front seat. The car wobbles while I start the engine, then we proceed toward the lake house our grandfather left us.

The ride is always silent when we have business to handle. I don't trust car speakers and technology, and I haven't had time to check the dead man for listening devices or a phone.

Sean lowers her seat back as far as it will go, and runs a pen through his pockets, between his legs, and around his ankles. She lifts herself back up and shakes her head side to side when she's done with the search.

The night fog on the lake is a blessing looking out for us when we arrive. I change into my rain boots from the trunk, and give Sean a pair of running sneakers. Together, we carry the body down to the boat. Sean starts it up while I collect bricks from the top of the mound that forms an entrance to the dock, and we travel to the middle of the lake where I start a small fire in a trash bin to burn my shirt, my victim's shirt splattered with blood, and the bag where the traces lie.

While the evidence burns, Sean ties bricks to his arms, while I tie them to his feet.

She squints. "I recognize him."

I gasp. "I don't. Who is he?"

"Three months back, we interviewed the woman from Seattle that asked to remain anonymous. This guy looks like the man who left the message demanding we erase her segment after it aired."

"What was the point? Neither of their names were disclosed."

Sean shrugs and twists her lips. "I'm guessing someone knows their story and knew it was about him."

I scoff. "These people never cease to amaze me. They lie, they cheat, and they harm, and then think they don't deserve any reckoning. You do people wrong, you gotta pay the price."

"What will our price be?"

I look at her used-to-be innocent face darkened with the moon floating behind her. "We paid in advance."

She doesn't challenge me.

I ask my devoted sister, "What did you think of the ladies tonight? Like *really* think of them?"

"Um. I think they were honest for the most part. I did notice Deja never said how her fella died. Though she did mention he crossed quite a few people."

"Which made it easy. He was so busy looking over his shoulder, he never saw me coming."

"You never told me how you did it."

"I'm not proud of that particular job. The less you know the better."

The fire wanes, and I collect the smoking embers

and ash then toss them into the lake. A few flakes sit on top of the water, defying to sink until we throw the man's body tied to the bricks on top of them.

The night is long, having to shampoo the seats and carpet in my car from top to bottom, vacuum it dry, and inspect for missed specks and strands of hair.

The drive back feels even longer as we sit in silence, listening to gospel music, both of us internally repenting.

Sean hops out. "See you in the morning."

"Sleep well."

"I'd say the same to you, but we both know you won't."

***

Visuals of the dead man, and the women's testimonies dance around in my head from the time I leave the studio to cleansing the day's sin off of me in the shower. I wrap my hair around a satin sock, moisturize my face before I slide into bed, and sit up against the headboard, bleeping out the names of the abusers from the recordings.

I feel that old tick in my mind become triggered at Kylah's ex-boyfriend, Clay Anthony. I rewind his name at least a dozen times, if not more, listening to the hurt in Kylah's voice when she says it the first time. Her words are clear, but when she spits out his name, it's said like a curse and stings like venom. I can taste the hatred she has for this half shell of a man as it transfers into me. I don't even know him and I hate him.

I sign into my backup PC and look up his name using my VPN. I want to buy the list of records attached to his name and read his entire manuscript of crimes, while the imagery of Kylah's face as she described the dents and broken glass of her car sends shooting pains in my chest.

I stare at the mugshot of a man I know is guilty of heinous crimes. A misfit with a long rap sheet of violent behavior, and disregard for women. A motherfucker I'd take pleasure in eliminating, unlike LaMar Wilkins who I almost felt something for in the end.

It was easy to get the attention of Deja's ex. Even easier to get him to agree to fuck me on a path off a dirt road at a hideaway house he visited from time to time.

I watched him for weeks. The many women he frequented. The house where he conducted business. The cars he rotated. The pharmacy where he picked up his pills.

"Oops." I bumped into him and knocked his bag out of his hand. "I'm so clumsy today." I reached for the bag and verified the name on the label. "Here you go." I handed it to him.

He took his prescription and groused. "You good,"
he said.

I smiled at him as I walked off, then looked back
at him one more time. Deja was honest about how good
looking he was. I began to understand how a gullible
girl could fall for his antics. Even I felt aroused when I
saw how he was looking at me.

As I left the store, he catcalled for me from his car.
I moseyed over to him and acted daft. He liked that I
appeared to be enamored by him.

He asked, "What you got going on for the rest of
the day?"

"That depends what you got going on?"

"Come take a ride with me."

"I'd rather follow you somewhere. I can't stand
being stuck without a car."

"I like a babe who likes having her own. Follow me
to my crib. We can kick it for the rest of the night."

When he turned down the road to his hideaway, I
flashed my lights. He pulled over to the side and I
made my play.

"I just got called in to work, so I can't kick it
tonight, but I do have a good twenty minutes to
spare." I slid my panties down from under my skirt
and dangled them on the edge of my finger.
"Get in."

He hopped in the back and unbuckled his jeans. I
climbed over my seat and mounted him.

"I didn't know I was gonna get lucky with you this fast," he said.

"You can thank the person who called out of work today. I never turn down overtime."

"I got your overtime right here." He thrusted against my leg.

I was tempted to take him as a lover before taking him out. I stared at him rolling down the condom, curious to feel him since we'd gotten this far, but then I looked into his eyes and saw the amount of women he'd visited since I began tailing him, and denied myself permission to explore the pleasure he'd been giving them.

My hands slipped under his shirt to feel up his chest. "Take this off," I said.

As he lifted it over his head, I reached for the needle in my bra, then pretended to help him remove it faster like I was overcome with lust, and stuck his arm with a sedative. He jumped with his shirt above his head.

"My nails got you." I kissed his chest. "I'm sorry."

He scowled. "That didn't feel like a nail."

I showed him my stiletto shaped nails. "See. I keep them sharp. Enough talking. I'm gonna be late for work."

I needed to buy time and throw him off my scent. I admit I took pleasure in reversing my earlier decision and inserted the good looking son-of-a-bitch inside of me. I indulged in the debauchery so many others have experienced with little regret. The feel of a man's touch I had sworn I would not indulge. The feel of this man in particular, stroking me as his eyes grew weak and weaker felt justified.

I pounced up and down on him to his liking until his hands fell limp and his johnson died inside of me. Gently, I slapped his face to see if he would wake. He mumbled and muttered, but couldn't open his eyes.

I then reached under the driver's seat and popped the cap on prescription pills identical to the ones he picked up every two weeks. I eased him out of me and covered his face with his shirt, then overdosed him until his consciousness faded into no pulse.

As I redressed him, I stared at him resting, waiting for remorse or regret to find me. I must have been invisible because I felt nothing as I watched this handsome man lay lifeless, wondering how he was still beautiful even in death.

I pulled my car next to his and struggled for a few minutes transferring his body into the driver's seat of his car. I collected the pills from his bottle and swiped the plastic bag from the store, left him secured in his car, then spun around the path a few times to obscure the tire markings.

On the open road, I tossed the condom into the grass. The closer I approached the town of Campo, I contemplated ditching the car in Lake Morena, but *the howls of coyote and my fear of viscous crawlers give me pause to walk the dark road.*

So, I sat tight in the 2011 Camry I stole from a bar outside of the city, and waited 'til daylight to trek to the bus station. Inside, the plastic bag from the pharmacy gets tossed in a restroom bin, and I used the phone at the front desk to call the local recycling center to pick up the car I abandoned on the side of the road.

The bus brought me back to Tucson where a cab delivered me to the cabin. I spent a few hours alone there before asking Sean to join me. And as always, she comes to my aid, no questions asked.

We reminisced about the good ole days until we fell asleep, and in the morning woke up to live another day.

The tick in my head grows louder as I think about LaMar's final moments. Then, a lightbulb goes off. I follow the idea and type a letter to Clay, offering to be a pen pal while he's serves his sentence. I sign it L.H. for Lonely Heart and bring it with me to the office in the morning.

Sean arrives, looking bright and shiny as she always does. Her youthful, sun-kissed skin is highlighted with makeup and red lipstick today. I smirk at her, recognizing she's come up with a plan. The red lipstick always makes an appearance when she's confident it'll work.

I greet her with my idea. "I started working on the inmate this morning."

"Good. What he did to Kylah was despicable. What's the play?"

"To become his friend. A confident on the outside. It's a long play I have in mind." I raise a brow. "I can tell you've come up with something yourself. Let's hear it."

She plops down in her chair opposite me and crosses her legs. "You're gonna like this one."

"Yeah?"

Her red lips part wide with a smile. "I found Mona Lisa's guy, Dwight."

"How positive are you it's the right one?"

"Still lives in Decatur, three-thousand-square-foot, two-story home in a neighborhood built roughly twenty years ago. Born in New York, married —no divorces. And judging from his wife's profile picture on socials, she looks how Mona Lisa described her, exotic, long, silky black hair." She hands me a Deskjet printed photo.

"*This him?*"

She nods. "Yup. It's him alright."

"He's decent looking. I can see why Mona Lisa fell for his bullshit when he was younger."

"I'm going to pretend I'm his long-lost daughter. I'll tell him I'm a private person and just want to meet my father before I permanently leave the country. Think he'll bite?"

"He might—especially to keep what he's been doing behind his wife's back from coming to the light. But we may not have to try so hard with him. I was thinking we should scope him out, see where he goes during the day, and you do that little thing you do when you're flirting to catch his attention."

"What thing?"

"That little puckering your lips out while twirling the end of your curls when you stare off into space. Men love when you do that."

She wipes the corner of her mouth. "I gotta find a new move."

"A young, pretty girl like yourself showing a man like him some attention...He'll come up with one of his best lines to go cheat on his wife."

"I'll do it."

"You get his number. Don't give him yours. And let's begin a thread. Given his history, trapping him should be easy like Sunday morning."

Sean chuckles. "Did you pull this plan out of your ass?"

"It came to me when you walked in. You and Mona Lisa share similar features. And now that I've seen the wife, it's obvious he likes petite, yellow women. The daughter story could lead to tricky questions such as years of conception and whatnot."

"I suppose you're right. You look well rested by the way."

"Looks can be deceiving. You and I know that."

She bounces from the chair and swipes the photo from my hand. "I sure do." She taps the photo. "Who would think looking at this sap he goes around serial cheating on his beautiful wife."

"Don't forget exposing women against their will to his demon seeds."

Sean slips his picture into the shredder. "I'll start looking for flights."

"Before you do, take a look at this." I hand her the note. "Give me the pros and cons of getting to know this one before we strike."

CHAPTER 11

SOPHIA

The podcast airs the usual disclaimer and a list of trigger warnings. Calls flood the office voicemail with praise for Kylah, Deja, and Mona Lisa's bravery to speak on their experiences. Comments begin to trend on social media about their testimony which run up the number of views.

"Wow. That Kylah lady was lucky to survive her ordeal."

"I don't think I could share such tragic events with the public. I'd be humiliated to let the world know if any of those things happened to me. I admire these women for lending their voice to bring awareness to the trauma women experience by simply being in a romantic relationship."

"Eye-opening episode. I learned so much about the different forms of abuse. It's scary to fall in love these days."

"I swear I dated each one of these guys. Why are men like this?"

"And this is why so many women are joining the 4B movement. And to think I use to be a Charlotte and wonder where is my knight in shining armor. Turns out, I'm it. #4BGIRLIE"

Sean checks in from Atlanta. Her recon work has been stellar in the past, so I'm not surprised when she delivers a thorough report.

"This Dwight guy is a real dirtbag, and he likes 'em young. He visits a woman in Buckhead when he leaves work. And this week, he went to happy hour on Tuesday. I find it odd that he goes to bars alone. Where are his friends?"

I add, "He does his dirt all by his lonely. Less mouths to spread his indiscretions."

"You know we didn't ask the ladies the dates of the stories they shared. Can you imagine this asshole's track record?"

"That just fueled me to hop on a plane. You feel like staying down there for a few more days?"

"Yeah. The food's good down here. I'll just lose the five pounds I'll probably gain when I come home."

I snicker. "I'll join you in the gym. But in the meantime, keep tailing him just in case anything changes. I'll fly into South Carolina Tuesday morning then drive to Georgia. I'm getting a good feeling about the happy-hour setting. Lots of ways to make something happen when the sun goes down. Fingers crossed he goes there next week."

"I'll text the list of hotels in the area."

"And I'll touch base when I arrive."

I park at a hotel down the road from Sean's location where a bus stop booth rests on the corner. With my hair tucked below a charcoal baseball cap resting above my eyes, I hop on the shuttle and make little to no eye contact with the other riders.

Five stops later, I hop off behind an elderly woman, slowly making her way toward a grocery store. I follow her across the street and veer from her side to visit a gas station in the shopping center's parking lot. I buy two burner phones, press my luck with a scratcher, then cure my munchies with a sandwich and soda from a food truck tucked away in the corner of the lot.

With a mouthful of food, I call Sean's hotel and ask to be transferred to her room.

I instruct her, "Buford Motel. Walk there. Key is under the mat on the passenger side. Drive five blocks toward the shopping center. You'll see me standing near chopped down trees, concrete, and orange tape draped on open land near a bus stop.

Twenty minutes later, I hop in the backseat like she's a rideshare, just in case I missed a camera.

"How far away are we from the girlfriend's house?"

"A good forty-five with traffic."

I slip Sean the second phone. "My number's in there. How long do we have until he arrives at her house?"

"Roughly two."

"And the happy hour spot?"

"Ten minutes south of her apartment."

"Take me there first."

I grin at the location when she rides by it. The club is perfect for the crime. A good ways out of the city, surrounded by woods, grass, and white gravel just off a main road. And if the lot is crowded, I'm covered to act quickly, and disappear in the mix. My getaway should be easy.

Then, Sean drives me to the apartment complex of the girlfriend.

"This won't do. There are cameras in those lights. More importantly, these people have Ring alarms on their doors."

Sean reaches to restart the car.

My hand covers hers. "Don't. Let me get a good look at him."

While we wait, we sort out our best laid plans. I offer Sean the other half of my sandwich.

She scowls. "You know I eat light the day of a job."

I stare at her with a side eye. "Or do you need a colonic after the way you've been eating down here?"

She laughs. "Two things can be true at once."

I smack my lips until they're clean. "Your loss. It's a really good sandwich. Something about the sauce."

Sean shakes her head at me, scratching her forehead. "I destroyed your letter to the inmate by the way. Too many factors will fuck us in the end nowadays. Guards read the mail, the phone calls are recorded, and what address would we use since they log everything that's incoming?"

"That's one of the *many* obstacles I've been trying to figure out. Technology is a gift and a curse."

"We've never done a prison run. What were you planning anyway?"

"To find out the roommate's name and convince him to do the deed for me."

"That would have been sweet. Our hands would be clean."

"It could have worked if shit wasn't digital nowadays."

"True. Video calls, scanned and stored correspondence, camera phones everywhere. We don't need anything leading back to us." Her voice softens into a whisper. "He's here. Five minutes early."

I snicker. "Why are you whispering? He can't hear us."

"Traffic must have been light today. Don't get me started on the hell I went through navigating through that fresh hell while trying to keep up with him."

"No complaints, Sis. It helped keep your cover."

"I guess."

The saying is true. Men get regal while women get haggard when they grow older. Dwight's salt and pepper strands on the edge of his receding hairline matched the shading in his goatee. I'm convinced it gives him an edge with the ladies, alongside the swagger in his walk that he is owning as he marches up to this woman's door.

He opens it with a key.

I shake my head as I smile. "And the wife doesn't suspect a thing?"

"Saw them at dinner the other night. Zero signs of conflict between them."

I glance at the nearby apartments. "These cameras have spared Mr. Dwight a few extra hours. Lucky bastard."

We press our luck and wait for him to arrive at the club. I lay low in the backseat while we sit in front of a mom-and-pop restaurant on the corner. He rolls past, and Sean cranks the car.

"Showtime," she says.

Sean circles the lot and gives me the coordinates

of where he's parked then situates us near the end away from the cameras. She hops out and I crawl to the driver's seat. She struts toward the entrance, kneels down to appear she is fixing her boot, and slips an AirTag in his rear tire.

I lean back and make myself comfortable with the windows cracked. Bass thumps into the lot, horny men brag of their intent for the evening as they walk past the car, and women stress their hopes of what they want to find inside.

"I hope these brokeys don't eat all the food this time," says a high-pitched voice.

"I know, right. Last time was a bust before seven," says her friend.

I grow antsy in the quiet when, finally, close to an hour later, the burner phone vibrates in my sweatshirt pocket. Noise from the inside rings in my ears: loud music, dishes flinging into a bucket, and men talking over other men begging for attention.

Faintly, I begin to hear a conversation between a woman and a man.

"How long are you gonna babysit that drink?" he asks.

A woman responds, "Why? You in some sorta rush?"

"I'm gonna be honest with you. I have a wife, and I'm out here just *tryna* fuck and go home. So what's up?"

'So he's morphed into an oxymoron. An honest cheat.'

"Damn. You're straightforward."

"I hear women like that."

"We do. But not so much the married part."

"Is that a deal breaker, 'cause I can pay?"

"How much you talkin'?"

"How much is it gonna cost me?"

"Walk me to my car, and let's discuss."

Sean mumbles through her teeth on the line. "Headed your way."

I slide on my gloves and observe Dwight leave the lot with the hookup close on his tail. I follow her car, keeping my distance, until it's time for all three vehicles to park outside a hotel near the interstate.

The lot has one spot available near the front entrance. The two of them exchange words before she takes it, and Dwight drives to the back lot, yards away from the safety lights and side door entrance.

He walks around to the front. I park the rental in reverse next to his car and wait for him to return. The fucker goes hard and long as it's been two hours he's had me on alert.

While he tests my patience, I call Sean to work out a new plan since Mr. Lover Lover has thrown us a curveball.

"Should we wait? It was easier to murk him outside the club," she says.

"Sometimes easy isn't best. If that were the case we could have run him off the road earlier, ya know. But you should definitely stay an extra day or two like we planned to CYA."

"And you?"

"I'm already in position. Just don't get rid of that phone until you track the AirTag is back in Tucson."

The alarm beeps and headlights flash on his car. I stand between our vehicles to block him when he walks up.

"Oh, hey." I cover my chest with my hands. "You scared me."

"Pardon me. I didn't mean to." He gives me a once-over then opens his car door. "How you doin'?"

I smile at him. "Good. How's your night?"

"Pretty decent, but there's still time for it to get better."

I click the button to open the trunk with the keyring. Dwight turns his head when it begins to rise.

"You need help with your b—"

I step in quick and slide my blade across his throat. His eyes meet mine, bugged out and wide. He grumbles a weakened cry and holds onto my hoodie, while scratchy notes squeeze out from his open mouth as he grasps for air.

As he clings to the last of his life, I shove him into the driver's seat of his SUV. One hand falls to his side while the other holds its grips on my sweatshirt. The burner phone falls into his lap, then he finally releases me when I reach for it.

He manages to croak out, "Why?"

"Karma," I answer. "Believe in her on your way out," I say, watching him take his last breath.

I secure his body upright with the seatbelt and insert a note that reads, *'You should have told me you were married'* on the floor next to his feet before locking him inside. I crawl to the rear tire and remove the AirTag, then pull off the gloves before I ease into my car and hop on the freeway.

I stuff the gloves, and burner phone inside the used sandwich bag while the full tank of gas drives me back to South Carolina. I switch my sweatshirt in the parking lot of the rental office, let my hair down, and stuff my cap in my carry-on.

The TSA tells me I can't carry my bag of food on the plane, so I trash it in the bin before walking through the scanner. I board my flight home and exhale once the wheels of the plane are up in the air.

Once we land, and I'm not greeted by officers when I exit the gate, I visit the ladies room and run the AirTag below water, then hide it inside a bag of pretzels from the plane. A Lyft takes me home where I burn everything—the sweatshirt, the hat, and my pants in the fireplace, and scorch the travel bag and my shoes inside a pile of leaves in the backyard.

In the morning, I dump the ashes into a trash bag

with soaked ammonia rags and the spoiled goods from the fridge. The garbage truck picks it up fifteen minutes later at the end of my driveway, and I sigh of relief as it buries my misdeeds below the loads of house waste it collects down the block.

Sipping on my coffee, I watch the neighbors leave their homes for work, the school bus pick up children, and the green truck roll out of the neighborhood, then dress to begin my day at the studio.

Sean calls. "Miss me yet?"

"I do. Find any interviews for us down there?"

"Not yet. How about you?"

"We're down one. But something will come along. See you when you get home."

Chapter 12

Sophia

The administrative duties for the show keep me busy all morning. Managing the schedule and comment sections on our socials is taxing without Sean. Responding to the positive support of our previous show that is producing our highest numbers to date with heart emojis, and blocking accounts from computer trolls afraid to show their faces is not how I imagined I'd spend the day. But I humor myself at the thought of tracking the trolls down to show them keyboard warriors aren't as invincible as they think.

The next day, Sean strolls into the office an hour before quitting time.

"Always good to see you, Sis. You have any trouble tying up loose ends?"

She hugs me. "Everything went according to plan, but for the love of God, I never want to fly out of Hartsfield airport again. How are you?"

"Good. Wanna take a walk?"

She nods, and we slide our phones to the center of the table.

We keep our voices low, and talk through our teeth behind forced smiles while on the street. Rushing winds, roaring engines, and beeping horns add to the noise audience.

Sean starts. "The local news hadn't reported anything before I left. I'll keep an eye out if the media decides he's worth covering."

"Any way to find out Average Joe's identity?"

"I messaged Mona Lisa and asked her for a follow-up. She declined. Says she was happy to share her voice and feels better with the weight of her story no longer holding her back from moving forward. She also said it's hard to read the negative comments."

"I've been deleting those all morning. A few rattled me to the point where I thought about making a surprise visit and slicing off those very fingers typing such bile."

Sean raises her brows.

"But I won't. Unless I have to," I mutter.

"Well I don't blame her. Some creeps have found her personal pages, telling her she deserved what happened to her."

I huff. "And that's why women don't come forward. Think about it. We interviewed three women, and not one of them called the law. In Deja's case, a man called the law for her, and she still didn't press charges." I kiss my teeth. "I don't blame Mona Lisa for choosing her peace. She's given us enough. I just wanted that other guy's name. Is she okay?"

"She said she's fine. She's privated her page and thanked us for giving her a platform."

"Do you think she's really fine?"

Sean stops at the ice cream shop and sends me a signal with her eyes that we should go inside. She orders our usual, cold brew cookie dough on a waffle cone and peanut butter fudge tracks.

I reach for my cone from the cashier. "Well?"

"I think she's telling the truth. I also think we made the right decision to expose those men. It's time the tables are turned, and we shift the narrative that victims should not be blamed for men's vile behavior, emotional dysregulation, and lack of self-control."

"I agree." I swallow a huge amount and speak before I fully swallow. "As for the inmate, it's going to be a while before he gets what he deserves."

She dips her spoon into her cup. "Those prison walls will have to serve as his karma for locking Kylah in that room against her will. We have no choice but to accept his sentence as justice...For now."

"For now." I sigh. "For now, he breathes. For now, he is free behind those bars, and he doesn't even know it. But rest assured, the moment he walks out of those gates, he better have made peace with his God, because *I will* bring him to his knees, and *he will* beg for mercy."

A breeze blows leaves at our feet. They dance in the formation of a windstorm creating a dust devil of nearby sticks, dirt, and grass.

"I think that's Mama telling us she approves what we're doing from the other side." Sean wraps her arm around me.

"She approves." I prim my lips forward. "If only we could have saved her."

The seasons change, but I don't. I begin classes at the shooting range in my spare time as the podcast has become a number one show. And with number one shows comes A-1 assholes. Most of them are men, but a few pick-mes leave nasty reviews every blue moon. They don't leave death threats like the online men gangstas, or tell me to off myself. They resort to insults toward the guests. Blaming them for being violated and repeating red pill content like mindless zombies that can't think for themselves.

My trusty blade can't handle a barrage of people coming at me at once, but a few bullets might help me survive if that day comes.

Sean and I split the load of fan and hate mail. We keep the hateful letters filed by arrival date just in case one of the crazies gets bold and brazen to act on their threat, and the fan mail gets added to our new wall of fame in the lobby.

Sean brings a post card to me. "This one doesn't have postage."

"Is it another threat?"

"No. It just says thank you."

She and I look at each other trying to read each other's mind.

"Could be anyone," I say.

"Should we test it for prints, hang it, or toss it?"

"Why would you suggest throwing it away?"

"I get a funny feeling about this one. Like someone kn..." Sean silences herself before completing her sentence.

"Then hang it. We might need it later." I slice open a few more letters and raise my brow at one from Kylah. "Sean. Looks like we have an update from Kylah." I read it to myself. "I could go for some ice cream."

Sean grabs her purse and the tape, then adds the postcard to the collage before we head to the parlor. She orders her usual. I surprise her and order a plain vanilla cone, and lead the way back outside.

"Vanilla? Since when?"

"Since I think you may be right someone possibly knows what we do. Kylah sent word that her ex has been paroled."

"Why tell us?"

"Exactly."

"I'll set up a call and find out if the ladies have been talking."

"And I'll see what I can find out about the day this asshole will be set free. The way I'm going to kill him will solidify my seat in hell."

REVIEWS
ENCOURAGE
VORACIOUS
INTEREST
EVERY
WHERE TO
SUPPORT

ME, THE AUTHOR

I GREATLY APPRECIATE IT

T.K. RICHARDS is a multi-genre author with popular novels and novellas in several genres of romance including Black, Interracial/Multicultural & Paranormal Romance, Speculative Fiction, Women's Fiction, and Domestic Thrillers. A graduate of Limestone University, T.K. has honors in Expository Writing, and was also the Poet Laureate of her graduating class. When she is not writing, she is immersed in the world of tennis, and binge watching movies—mostly comedy as she loves to laugh.

For more information about **T.K. Richards**, visit her website at www.tkrichards.com and subscribe to her newsletter at: https://tkrichardsnewsletter.ck.page

Follow **T.K. RICHARDS** on the platforms listed below to interact with her personally:

instagram.com/t.k.richards

pinterest.com/TKWrites

tiktok.com/@tkrwrites

youtube.com/tkrichards

goodreads.com/T.k.richards

bookbub.com/authors/t-k-richards

amazon.com/author/Tkrichards

patreon.com/tkrichards

bsky.app/profile/tkrichards

An Affair Abroad
T.K. RICHARDS

A TASTE
OF THE
Forbidden
T.K. RICHARDS

Blend
T.K. RICHARDS

T.K. RICHARDS
STRAIGHT LINE

T.K. RICHARDS
DERAILED

T.K. RICHARDS
THE CROSSING

JUKE
T.K. RICHARDS

Lowcountry
Legends
tk richards & dana richard

THE
Vampiress
T.K. RICHARDS

Still
not over
YOU
T.K. RICHARDS

Mikki
&
Mason
T.K. RICHARDS

EN
ROUTE
TO
EMERY
A Novel
T.K. RICHARDS

MY GIFT
TO
You
T.K. RICHARDS

T.K. RICHARDS
CAN'T
QUIT
You

SINS
of
THE
MOTHER
T.K. RICHARDS

* 9 7 8 1 9 5 9 2 5 3 2 5 9 *